The Trouble with Perfect

By Christy Barritt

Other Books by Christy Barritt

Squeaky Clean Mysteries:
#1 Hazardous Duty
#2 Suspicious Minds
#2.5 It Came Upon a Midnight Crime
#3 Organized Grime
#4 Dirty Deeds
#5 The Scum of All Fears

Suburban Sleuth Mysteries:
#1 Death of the Couch Potato's Wife

Love Inspired Suspense:
Keeping Guard
The Last Target
Race against Time
Ricochet
Key Witness
Lifeline
High-Stakes Holiday Reunion (November 2013)

Stand-alone Novels:
The Good Girl
Home Before Dark

Nonfiction:
Changed: True Stories of Finding God through Christian Music
The Novel in Me: The Beginner's Guide to Writing and Publishing a Novel

This book is dedicated to small towns across the United States. You're a treasure that always gets my creativity flowing.

A special thanks goes out to Kathy Applebee and Pat Mathias for their help with this book.

Chapter One

I remember the day that darkness slithered into my home. Like a boa constrictor, evil wrapped itself around the very heart of our family and squeezed until all signs of life were gone.

The words replayed in Morgan Blake's mind.

Thirty-three words down. Only 74,967 more to go, she reminded herself.

In forty days.

The realization nagged at Morgan. Made her unable to sleep. Caused her to eat in binges.

That opening line was all she had for her new novel, and it was all she'd had for the past year.

Out of desperation, she'd decided to try a change of scenery to get her creative juices flowing. Being in this house provided too many reminders of the tragedy that occurred two years ago. Too many painful memories and too much grief.

"Are you sure you're going to be okay on this trip?"

Tyler Carlson stood beside her little red sports car, the breeze trolling over the sand dunes from the ocean and devilishly ruffling his brown hair. Morgan stood in front of him, a suitcase at her feet and her heart in her throat. Why did she feel so hesitant to leave?

"I think this is going to be good for me. I've been…"

"Secluded?"

She shrugged. "I was going to say stuck in a rut."

He bent his head, his brown eyes warm with compassion. "We've all noticed that you've been distant since Braden died. We're worried about you."

"You're a saint, Tyler. Most people would have given up on me by now."

"I'll never give up on you, Morgan."

The sincerity in his voice made her oddly aware of her pounding heart. "You're a sweetheart."

"A saint. A sweetheart. Any other compliments you want to throw my way before this trip?"

Morgan grinned. "I don't know about compliments. How about...overprotective. Hard-headed. Way too patient for a normal person—"

Tyler chuckled and held up his hand. "Okay, okay. I should have let you stop while I was ahead." His grin slipped. "You sure I can't go with you? I could see if there are some extra rooms at the bed and breakfast..."

Morgan grabbed a loose strand of her honey-colored hair and wrapped it behind her ear. "You act like I'm going into a war-torn country known for taking Americans hostage. I'm going to West Virginia, and I'm going to be fine. I'm not a child."

"I realize that."

What was that look in his eyes? Regret? Affection? Morgan couldn't read the emotion—or maybe she didn't want to read it. Instead, she took a slow step back and nodded toward her car. "I've gotta run."

"I'd feel better if you could at least give me the name of the town where you're going."

—

6

Details were never quite her thing. Which is why she should probably hire an assistant, as everyone kept urging her to do. It was just that she enjoyed her privacy so much.

She held up a paper. "I've got directions."

"Normal people would use a GPS."

"You think I'm normal? I thought you knew me better than that."

"No comment." He grinned. "I just don't understand your resistance to using technology to help you find where you're going."

"I just want to throw the thing out my window when that voice starts telling me where to go. And that's on a good day."

He held up his hand in surrender. "Okay, okay. I get it. Just call me when you get there."

"You're always looking out for me, aren't you?" He'd been good to her over the past two years. What had started as Morgan dog-sitting for him while he worked his shift had turned into daily walks and surprise visits with supper in hand.

"Someone's got to do it."

Morgan couldn't deny the fact that, if it wasn't for Tyler, she could disappear and no one would probably notice for at least a week. Oh, maybe her literary agent would notice something wrong when she called to find out the status of Morgan's supposed work-in-progress. Of course, Morgan had been avoiding her phone calls lately, so even her agent might not get suspicious.

She reached up and pecked Tyler's cheek with a kiss. "I appreciate you. I do. And I'll be fine. Don't worry about me. Go and have some fun without me here to tie you down. Ask out that lady who just moved in next door. She's always asking about you and batting her mascara-laden eyes when you're around."

"I'll pass."

Morgan couldn't remember the last time Tyler actually dated someone… probably since before Braden died. Her fiancé's death had affected more than just Morgan. Tyler had been his best friend, and he obviously had no idea what to do with himself anymore. It was the only excuse Morgan could think of as to why he would hang out with her so much.

She reached through the open car window and grasped the inside latch of her door. The outside handle was broken. Another detail of her life that she'd neglected lately.

"You really need to get that fixed," Tyler said.

She nodded as she slid into the car and slammed the door. "It's on my list."

Tyler leaned on her open window. "I'll be waiting to hear from you."

Morgan cast him good-natured grin. "I know."

She pushed her sunglasses over her eyes and glanced at Tyler once more. The former University of Virginia quarterback stretched his broad, muscular frame to full height as he backed away from her car. She was really blessed to have a friend like him. She couldn't deny that.

She started down the beach-front road, noting the sand that had spilled over the dunes after a late-night thunderstorm yesterday. Today, the sun shone brightly against a brilliant blue sky. It seemed to promise her trip would be a success. She prayed it would be.

Morgan was working on her fourth novel. Her first three had been surprising successes and, when a production company had picked up the first book and made it into a movie, her popularity soared. That, coupled with morning talk show rounds and magazine interviews, had propelled Morgan into the kind of success she'd only dreamed about. But now her readers, and her editor, were demanding another book and all of her recent ideas had seemed to fizzle out before the words even reached paper.

All she had was that opening line that seemed to taunt her. *I remember the day darkness slithered into my home.* She had to start her novel with that line. She didn't know why. She just knew there was a story there, waiting to be explored.

She willed herself not to think about writing for the moment. There would be plenty of time for that once she got to West Virginia. For now, she just wanted to enjoy the drive from Virginia Beach.

As cars zoomed past on the interstate, she looked beyond them to the landscape. It slowly changed from flat wetlands to woodsy rolling hills and finally majestic mountains laden with the colors of fall. Cities were scarce. It was mostly farmland dotted with cows, horses, and long expanses of wooden fences. As the sun began to drop over the horizon, the temperature slipped from comfortable to brisk.

Morgan punched a button and the radio came on. She hurried past country music, oldies and commercials, finally pausing at a captivating melody.

"You are my strong tower, my refuge and shield," a baritone sang amidst guitars and catchy drumbeats.

God a strong tower and refuge? She supposed there had been a time in her life when she'd believed that. Now, he seemed more like a controlling authoritarian who continuously dangled happiness just out of her reach. She still believed in him. She still prayed, even. But she just couldn't think of him as loving and kind and protecting. She flipped the station and settled on some acoustic rock instead.

As she approached the West Virginia state line she reviewed her plans for the week. The first thing on her agenda was a book signing in a small town. She'd received the invitation a month earlier and found it impossible to resist. Her novel, "Redemption's End," was a legal thriller set in a small West Virginia town. The letter requesting her to visit and do a book signing had tugged at her heartstrings in such a way that she couldn't say no.

We're a small town often neglected by the rest of the world. Hard times have fallen on us with the economy, but your book and its message has brought us a spark of hope. It would mean so much to our town's morale if you'd visit...

She hadn't done a book signing in awhile. In fact, since Braden's death she'd been a marketing nightmare, though no one would confront her with that truth. She knew, though. Her previous job had been in public relations, so she knew what was expected of her if she wanted to be the media darling so many envisioned her being.

She'd gone full-time with her writing after "Redemption's End" had released at theaters. The all-star cast had made the movie number one at the box office for three straight weekends and secured Morgan a comfortable future. She had a name now, and names tended to sell books. Most people looked at her life and thought it was perfect. They didn't realize the inner demons she struggled with.

A wailing siren from a police car zooming past brought her back to the present. As she weaved between traffic, she plotted out her trip. First she'd do the book signing and stay at the housing already set up for her. Then she'd look for a cozy bed and breakfast nearby—maybe one surrounded by woods and with a little babbling brook outside—where she could relax and enjoy herself. *Not to mention, to write my book,* she reminded herself. Though she tried to push those thoughts to the back of her mind, they pushed themselves forward nonetheless.

This was her first experience with writer's block. Her first three books had come so easily. The ideas had required little effort and the characters had taken on a life of their own. She simply went where the characters in the book took her. If only it was that easy this time.

Grabbing the piece of paper she'd laid on the passenger's seat, she read the directions to the bookstore. The directions seemed simple enough—an exit number, a left turn, thirty miles on the same road, and then a few turns at the end. Though she avoided using a GPS at all costs, certain times — like now — she questioned her stubbornness.

Her exit neared. Turning her radio down, she paid careful attention to the road signs. Moments later she turned off the interstate onto a surprisingly barren exit. She picked up the directions and double-checked them. She hadn't made any wrong turns.

With one last glance at the paper, she continued farther into the heart of the mountains.

***

Morgan had taken off her sunglasses over an hour ago. The directions that Bonnie — the owner of the bookstore — had given her weren't accurate. That fact, mixed with Morgan's bad sense of direction, made for trouble. She'd tried her cell phone, but there was no signal out here. As the darkness grew deeper, the knot in Morgan's stomach twisted even tighter.

It had been more than an hour since she'd seen the one and only street sign, so her map was rendered useless. The trees and the mountains she'd once thought of as peaceful and relaxing now seemed looming and creepy.

Things were not going according to plan.

"Didn't I just pass that mountain?" Morgan muttered. Maybe her mind was playing tricks on her. Maybe not.

She gripped the wheel tightly as anxiety knotted in her neck. A wall of rock stood menacingly to her right, making her all too aware of the steep drop off to her left. As she rounded another sharp curve, Morgan sat up straighter, easily imagining rounding one of these bends and hitting a deer or some other large mammal. Morgan would have gladly traded rush hour traffic any day to this stuff.

Her headlights illuminated the asphalt in front of her, casting light into the blackness. Her foot hovered over the brakes, ready to slam on the pedal at the first sign of trouble. Trouble? Her imagination was working overtime. She just needed to relax.

She flipped her radio station back on, hoping some music would calm her down. Instead, all she heard was static. *Static? Really? There's got to be some kind of radio station out here.* She plucked the radio dial in frustration before looking up.

Out of nowhere, a man appeared in the road, directly in front of her. Morgan's heart knotted. "No!"

She slammed on her brakes. The car swerved. Out of control, the Miata careened dangerously close to the edge of the road, to the cliff.

The man bounced across the hood. His face smeared against the windshield. Morgan's scream pierced the air as the car finally stopped moving.

Her hand flew over her mouth as she stared at the face only inches from her own, separated by a thin wall of glass. She struggled to get her breath. Was the man dead? Had she just killed someone?

Adrenaline took over. Morgan reached for the door. She had to see if the man was okay.

Just then, the man's eyes pulled open.

He stared at her with wide, dazed eyes. A frantic look seemed to emanate from him, as if he were scared and crazed at the same time. He remained motionless for a moment, his blinking eyes the only sign he was alive.

Morgan stared at him breathlessly, waiting to see what would happen next. She frantically took in the man's wild, blond hair that fell into his rugged, tanned face. The white baseball hat worn backwards.

Blood drizzled from his nose and his breathing was heavy. But he was alive! Her heart rate slowed for a moment.

The man slowly lifted his face from the windshield and formed a single word with his mouth.

Morgan blinked, trying to decipher what he said. He mouthed the same word again.

"Help," she whispered shakily. "He needs help."

She jerked the door open. At the same moment, the man lifted himself from the car and darted into the woods.

And, as if it had never happened, he was gone.

Chapter Two

Morgan sprinted to the edge of the road. The man somehow managed to pull himself off of her car, dart across the road, and into the woods where the road steeply dropped off.

Squinting, Morgan peered through the forest. Despite the semi-darkness of early evening, she fully expected to see the man's body crumpled on the ground nearby. Instead all she saw was the ghostly outline of some trees. There wasn't a body to be found.

"Hello?" she called out into the unknown.

She listened for a response. All that answered were her echo, the songs of the wilderness, and the earthy smell of dried, crisp leaves. She heard no limbs breaking, no leaves crumbling, no twigs snapping beneath the weight of an unexpected guest.

A shiver ran through her. It could have been from what had just happened or from the chilly mountain air. Most likely it was both. She pulled her arms around herself.

"Okay." She took a deep breath. "I'm going to stay calm. I can handle this."

At that very moment she desperately wished Tyler was here. He would know exactly what to do and how to handle this situation. And something about his presence always made her feel safe. He was one of the few men in her life she could say that about. Maybe she should have let him come with her on this trip.

"The police," she said. "I should call the police."

As she rushed back to her car, the dent in her hood caught her eye. Seeing it brought her a measure of comfort. At least she hadn't imagined everything. In the same sense it was disarming. Had all of this really just happened?

Without wasting more time, she jumped into her car and pulled out her cell phone to call 911.

"Come on!" She hit the cell phone with the palm of her hand. The basic message didn't change —no signal. She'd contemplated getting a new phone service for months now. Why hadn't she? It left her with only one choice — to drive until she found somewhere with either a sheriff or a phone. She couldn't stay where she was. The likelihood of someone driving past was slim.

Putting her car in drive she tried to shake off the uneasiness, feeling like a horse that had been spooked. *Lord, please help me to find civilization!*

She continued on the treacherous mountain road. As she rounded a curve, a building came into view. She had to blink twice to make sure she was seeing correctly. Sure enough, another building appeared and then another and another. Relief flooded through Morgan. She'd found a town. A real town.

"Thank You, Lord," she whispered. "I needed this."

Her eyes scanned the street signs, searching for one that would identify the Sheriff's Office. The town itself didn't look very large. It consisted of only a few blocks of shops and offices and houses.

Finally, at a building at the end of the last block, she saw the sign reading "Sheriff's Office." She pulled to a stop, turned off her car and hurried across the sidewalk, all too aware of how vital time was in this situation. She scrambled up the front steps and grabbed the brass door handle. With a tug, she tried to jerk it open. The door wouldn't budge. It was locked.

This had to be a mistake. Sheriff's Offices didn't close, did they? Leaning her head against the door, she tried to think of another plan of action.

The face of the man she'd hit flashed through her mind. What if he was lying in the woods with a broken arm or fractured ribs or a concussion? The longer it took to get someone out there, the worse the situation was going to be. The more likely the man might ... die? Morgan shuddered.

She surveyed the street, searching for a sign of life. Nobody was in sight. Not only that, she didn't see any pay phones and all the shops appeared to be closed. This was getting more awful by the minute. She had to find help and quickly. The urgency of the situation made her jittery.

"Is everything okay?" a masculine voice asked behind her. "Can I help you with something?"

Morgan whirled around. A well-dressed man stood on the sidewalk, a briefcase in his hands and curiosity across his aristocratic face. She quickly assessed him. Early forties, dark hair, intelligent eyes. Since she had no other options, this man would do.

"I need help," she rushed. "I need the sheriff. It's an emergency. Someone could be hurt."

The man nodded, his eyes seeming to assess her sense of urgency. "An emergency, you said? Then, by all means, his home's just up the street. Allow me."

"Thank you." Morgan fell into step beside him.

They began walking uphill on the sidewalk to a row of homes in the distance. Perhaps it was the accident or the fact she was walking with a stranger in a strange town without another soul in sight, but something caused goose bumps to spread across her skin. She wrapped her arms over her chest.

Morgan cleared her throat. "I really appreciate this."

"It's not a problem." The man turned toward her, his shoes still clicking against the smooth sidewalk. "By the way, my name is Gavin. Gavin Antoine."

Common courtesies. She'd forgotten about them. She attempted a smile. "I'm Morgan."

"Would that be Morgan Blake? The Morgan Blake?" His blue eyes flickered in surprise.

"The one and only." Wry amusement caught her voice. Her popularity hadn't earned her any favors tonight.

The man's gaze swept back to her, concern in his eyes. "Whatever's happened has shaken you."

Morgan simply nodded. She needed to tell the sheriff what happened first, not this man, despite how kind he'd been. Their footfalls against the sidewalk filled the silence.

"You've been the talk of the town this week," Gavin finally offered. One hand seemed to be almost debonairly stuffed into his pocket while the other gripped his leather briefcase. A business man. What was a businessman doing out this hour? In this town?

"This isn't exactly the way I planned my arrival." The injured man's face flashed in her mind, rekindling the immediacy of the situation. Morgan stepped up her pace. She had to get to the sheriff's house soon.

"You look like you've seen a ghost."

Morgan closed her eyes, warding away the memories. "I think maybe I have." She stopped walking and settled her gaze on Gavin. "I got lost on my way here. It was dark and I was frustrated. I came around the corner and, out of nowhere, there was a man in the road …" The story poured out of her before she had time to check herself.

Gavin listened, lines of concern forming on his forehead. "That sounds terrible. Don't worry, Ms. Blake. Everything's going to be okay. We'll get someone out there to check everything out."

A calming reassurance saturated his voice. He maintained eye contact with Morgan until her breathing steadied. Then they began walking again.

"Thank you," she said again, her voice low. "I'm a little flustered right now."

"As anyone would be in your situation. Just continue taking deep breaths. We're almost at the sheriff's house."

Morgan heeded his advice and maintained her breathing. When they arrived at a skinny, two-story home, her nerves had settled some. The sheriff answered the door, still in uniform and with a toothpick between his teeth. Gavin introduced her to Sheriff Lowe, a man with a bulbous tummy, ruddy skin and a gold front tooth.

"Gavin." The sheriff shifted beady eyes from Morgan to Gavin. "What can I do for you?"

"This young lady needs some help. Seems there was an accident of sorts she was involved with outside of town."

The sheriff stepped back from the door to allow them inside. "Why don't you tell me what happened?"

Morgan recounted the story again. Sheriff Lowe nodded and grunted at each new piece of information. When she finished, Gavin turned to Sheriff Lowe.

"I take it you'll get some men on it?" Gavin said.

"Right away. We'll need you to take us to the scene, ma'am."

"Of course," Morgan said.

"Very well." Lowe released a big breath of air. "Let me just get my deputies on the phone and we'll drive out there." He reappeared a moment later with hat in hand, ready to go.

They walked outside to his police car. Morgan climbed into the passenger's seat. She noted that Gavin climbed into the back of the police car also, but didn't question it. She had bigger questions at the moment. Life or death questions.

"Describe the man you say you hit." The sheriff cruised down the road. Couldn't he go any faster? She had to get a grip. Not everyone in law enforcement was untrustworthy. Like Tyler, for example. She could trust Tyler.

Morgan told him everything she could remember. When she finished, the sheriff turned to Gavin. "Doesn't really fit the description of anyone here, does it?"

Gavin leaned forward from the backseat. "I can't say he sounds familiar."

"You say he just ran back into the woods?" The sheriff's gaze flickered toward her.

Morgan nodded. "For a moment, I thought he might be dead. The next moment he sprinted from my car hood."

"Legally, you won't have any obligations if the man has run away," the sheriff said. "For starters, it was an accident. Secondly, the young man didn't stick around to pursue anything further."

"Legal obligations or not, my heart won't let me rest until I know if he's okay." Morgan eyed the road before her. "It was somewhere in this area. There should be skid marks. I'm sure there are because I slammed on my brakes."

Sheriff Lowe slowed. Morgan's eyes focused on the cliff to their left as the car's headlights illuminated the area. As the road curved she recognized the spot where the accident happened. "Right here!"

Before the sheriff brought his car to a halt, Morgan had practically exited and scrambled toward the origin of the accident. She scanned the road, looking for evidence of the crash. There had to be something.

She blinked at the eerily empty roadway. She leaned down and ran a finger against the asphalt. It was wet. Why was the road wet?

Gavin seemed to read her mind. He pointed to a tiny stream of water trickling down the mountainside and across the road. In the dark she hadn't noticed it. Morgan nodded in understanding. "Of course. But shouldn't there still be skid marks?"

"Perhaps they are very faint and we won't be able to detect them until daylight."

"So, where did this John Doe disappear into the woods?" The sheriff stepped forward.

Morgan closed her eyes, trying to remember the scene. When she opened them she walked to the edge of the road and pointed down. The vast wilderness stood taunting before her, feeling like an animal waiting to pounce. Fresh air wafted upward, but Morgan knew better than to be deceived by its sweet allure. She pointed right into the heart of the darkness. "Right here. He shot from my car straight into the woods. I got out of the car and called for him, but there was no answer."

The sheriff nodded. "I'll have my men search the woods when they get here."

"I just don't understand why he would run away like that," Morgan whispered. "It doesn't make sense."

"People do unusual things when they're under a great amount of stress or trauma," Gavin said. "It was probably his adrenaline taking over."

How do you know all of this? Morgan wanted to ask. *And why does the sheriff keep looking to you for direction?*

Another sheriff's cruiser came around the curve with its lights flashing and screeched to a halt. Two deputies scrambled over each other to reach Sheriff Lowe. Morgan had the sinking feeling these small town officers were more amateurish than she'd feared. A knot twisted in her stomach. Could she trust the Barney Fife wannabes to find the man she hit? Did she have any other choice?

"Okay, we're going to split up and cover this area of the woods." Sheriff Lowe tucked in his shirt and waddled forward, pointing to several of his men with chubby fingers. "We're looking for a young man who may be injured. Based on the way Ms. Blake described what happened, I'd guess he didn't make it very far."

The sheriff went on to explain how they would divide up before releasing the deputies to start searching.

Morgan stood in beams of the headlights from the sheriff's car for a moment, feeling at a loss. Finally, she snapped out of her stupor and stepped forward. "How about me? I want to help search, too."

The sheriff glanced at Gavin as if to get his permission before answering. Morgan carefully watched the exchange, curious about the silent messages being spoken. Gavin nodded—but barely— before looking back at her with a disarming, yet subdued grin.

Sheriff Lowe turned toward Morgan. He licked his lips and heaved in a deep breath. "It would be best if you stayed here, ma'am. The wilderness is no place for a woman at night."

Indignation surged through her, causing her to stand ramrod straight. "You don't understand. I'm going to help look for this man. It's my fault he's injured. I'm not going to stand by doing nothing when he could be hurt."

Gavin's hand covered her arm, as if he could sense the rising tension in Morgan. "I'll walk with you and we can check along one of the tamer trails. We really should let the deputies trudge through that underbrush. Neither of us is dressed for it, and you don't want to get lost out there. Believe me, it's happened before, and there's not always a happy ending."

Morgan's throat went dry. Hauling through the forest at this hour wasn't her ideal either, but she couldn't live with herself if she didn't do everything possible to help that man. "I'm up for it."

Gavin tugged off his sport jacket and loosened his tie before reaching out his hand to the sheriff. "Do you have an extra flashlight?"

The sheriff nodded toward his cruiser. "In the glove compartment. Meet us back here in two hours. Otherwise, I'll be sending out another search party."

Gavin went to the car and came back with a flashlight. Then he and Morgan strode several feet down the road until they came to a trail that cut through the woods.

Morgan wasn't used to the darkness, a force so thick it nearly seemed material. In the city, she was lucky to

---

24

see even a glimmer from the stars. The night wasn't so dark there and the quiet of the city seemed noisy in comparison to the silence of the mountains around her.

"We have several trail systems that cut through the hills around here. It's not unusual for backpackers or white-water rafters to spend time here. They're mainly the ones to use these trails." Gavin darted the flashlight all around them, searching for something that would give them a clue as to what had happened to the man Morgan hit.

"Under different circumstances, I might actually enjoy this hike," Morgan said.

Gavin smiled, his teeth flashing in the darkness. Or had she only imagined the glint of white?

Gavin continued. "It's still too dark to see much now, but it's quite a lovely walk during the morning hours. The sunlight streams through the branches of the trees, creating an almost enchanting effect. The dew makes everything glimmer. And, if you keep on the trail long enough, you'll run into a river at the base of the mountain."

"Sounds like you know this trail pretty well."

"We're a small community out here. There's not much to do, so you learn to appreciate what's around you."

"How close is the nearest town?"

"Forty-five minutes."

Morgan blinked in surprise. "I have to admit I didn't know there were places this secluded that existed anymore. I didn't think I'd ever find my way here."

—

Gavin laughed softly again. "We kind of like being nestled away here in the mountains. It has its advantages."

"I'm sure it does."

They walked for a few minutes in silence. The trail wasn't steep but winding. Around them the forest loomed, its branches reaching out to grab them on occasion. When they had walked an hour, they turned around to start back. Their search had yielded nothing. Morgan's heart sank.

Gavin seemed to sense her mood. "Maybe one of the others found him."

"It just doesn't seem like he could have gone very far. He has to be injured…"

"I'm sure if the sheriff doesn't find anything tonight that he'll search again when it's daylight."

They were the first ones to arrive at the cluster of cars alongside the road. Maybe that meant that the others had found something. The sound of someone trudging through the underbrush caused goose bumps to prickle her skin. A moment later, two deputies arrived—empty handed. The sheriff appeared a few seconds later.

The moisture left Morgan's throat. "Nothing?"

When they shook their heads, Morgan swayed, the darkness suddenly blurry and overwhelming.

Why had the man asked for help and then run away? And how was she ever going to give him any help if they couldn't find him?

Chapter Three

Gavin's hand cupped her elbow to steady her. His touch brought her back down to reality.

"It's going to be okay, Morgan."

Why did she feel like she'd known this man much longer than she actually had? The realization unnerved her and she straightened, causing Gavin to step away. Great, she'd just offended the one man who'd been kind to her since she arrived. She'd deal with that later.

Morgan locked gazes with the sheriff. "What's next? Search some more? Call in some back up? The state police?"

The sheriff hiked his pants up over his overflowing waist. "It would be best if we just waited until the morning to continue the search."

Waited? Certainly Morgan hadn't heard correctly. She raised her palms in the air, outrage flowing through her limbs and all the way to her fingertips. "But what if he's hurt? He could be dying out there for all we know."

Sheriff Lowe licked his cracked, peeling lips as he drew himself up to full height. "I can't endanger the life of my men. These mountains are dangerous. The most logical thing is to wait until the morning."

"Maybe I should just go and look for him myself!
It's better than what you're doing, which is nothing!"
She took a step—an angry step, if there was such a
thing—toward the tree line when a firm hand gripped
her arm.

She jerked her head up and saw Gavin. His eyes
seemed to plead with her. "That wouldn't be a good
idea. Then we'd simply have two missing persons
instead of one. Listen to the sheriff. How injured could
the man be if he escaped from the basic search area?"

"Escaped?" Morgan shuddered as she said the
word.

Gavin's grip loosened. "Bad word choice. But you
know what I mean."

Did she? Could she settle for waiting? Gavin did
have a point—she would most likely only get lost
herself out in that wilderness. Her skin crawled at the
thought. Finally, she nodded. "You're right. I'll trust
law enforcement to do their job."

Gavin nodded, the action steady and confident.
"Smart thinking. How about we get you back to your
car and settled into town for the night? This was not the
welcome we anticipated giving you here in town."

Sucking in a deep breath, she attempted to compose
herself and lighten the situation—as if that was
possible. "You don't know of any all night pancake
houses around here, do you?"

The apple she'd eaten on the way wasn't enough
any longer. Maybe something to eat would help clear
her head and think clearly.

"None of those around here, but I think I could find a place where something could be whipped up for you."

Morgan shook her head. "I don't want to be any trouble."

"Ms. Blake, you're our guest of honor. It wouldn't be any trouble. Besides, if Bonnie were to find out I let you go hungry, she'd have my head on a platter. She's the bookstore owner and one of your biggest fans."

"Yes, I remember Bonnie. Her letter was quite persuasive." She drew in a deep breath, contemplating what to do. She finally went with her hunger. "Okay then, I accept."

"We'll search again in the morning, Ms. Blake," Sheriff Lowe said. "Sometime tomorrow, if you could stop by the office, we'll write up an official report. Until then, I'll drop you two off to get something to eat."

"I appreciate that."

Five minutes later the sheriff stopped along the store-lined street. Morgan shivered as she glanced at the quiet town around her. She was at the mercy of a place where she knew no one and where she'd been forced to rely on the kindness of a stranger. At the moment, she felt small and isolated.

"Ms. Blake?" Gavin stood at the door of a restaurant named Donna's.

"Is Donna your wife?" Morgan looked up at the quaint wooden sign above the storefront.

"No, I'm not married, Ms. Blake. I actually bought this eatery from Donna a few years back. She was about to go under, so I decided to help her out. She still runs it. I just kind of oversee everything that goes on."

Gavin unlocked the door and pushed it open for Morgan to enter before following behind her and flipping on the lights. The interior of the restaurant came into view, a surprisingly modern space with a rich tile floor and solid wood tables. The eatery seemed almost out of place. As did Gavin.

She looked him over as he walked into the kitchen. He wore a designer suit, fitted for his measurements. His wavy black hair, sprinkled with a few slivers of gray, was well groomed. His movements showed grace and ease. His smile had a movie-star quality about it.

"How about a sandwich?" he called from behind the counter.

Morgan pulled out a barstool and sat across from him. "Sounds great."

"Any requests?"

"Anything you'll make me." She continued to study him, allowing her mind to drift from the accident. She guessed Gavin to be in his early forties. His body was slender and toned, not to mention tanned. When he spoke, his accent wasn't West Virginian, but he had a slight Northeastern crispness to his words.

"May I ask what you're thinking, Ms. Blake?" He glanced over his shoulder at her as he pulled out some bread and cheese from the refrigerator.

"I'm trying to figure out how you ended up in a place like this. And speaking of this place, does this town have a name?"

"Perfect." He walked back toward the counter with some bread and lunchmeat, not missing a step as he said the word.

Morgan tilted her head. "Perfect? What do you mean?"

He lifted a butter knife, his eyes sparkling. "The town you are in at this moment is Perfect, West Virginia."

Morgan blinked twice. She then nodded, marveling at the name. "Perfect, huh? I like that. The town's so small it doesn't show up on any maps, does it?"

Gavin assembled the bread and cheese with precision before pushing the plate her way. "No, I guess it doesn't. We like it that way." He paused, leaning with his hands against the countertop. "Drink?"

"Any kind of soda. Not diet. Preferably with caffeine." She picked up the sandwich before her and took a bite. The turkey on wheat bread satisfied her. Gavin returned a moment later and placed a drink before her.

"This is perfect," she said, wiping the corners of her mouth with a napkin.

"As is the town." He grinned.

Morgan let out a small laugh. "I can tell you have fun with that one. You never did tell me where you were from."

"Boston." He placed both hands on the counter and looked at her with a sparkle in his eyes, waiting to see her reaction.

"And how did you end up here?"

"I've always liked the mountains and small towns. Never was much of a city boy."

Something about Gavin's gaze captivated Morgan. She'd been so preoccupied earlier with the accident that she hadn't noticed how beautiful his eyes were. They were an amazingly clear shade of blue, one that matched the ocean near her home. When they caught her gaze, it felt like a trance came over her. She pulled away before she looked like a lovesick schoolgirl staring at him.

She washed down the last bite of her sandwich with her soda and leaned back. "I can't thank you enough for everything you've done for me. I mean, I am a stranger and you've taken me under your wing. I don't know what I would have done if I hadn't run into you."

"I don't think that us running into each other was a mistake." He caught her gaze. "There is a reason for everything."

She raised her eyebrows, surprised by his implications. "I agree."

A smile lit his face. "Why don't we go sit over in one of the booths for a little while and have some coffee? The bed and breakfast is closed. We'll have to wake up the owner at this point, any way we look at it."

Morgan glanced at her watch and gawked at the time. 11:15. Nearly midnight. "Is it really that late?"

"I'm afraid it is."

Morgan settled into a booth while Gavin poured two cups of coffee from the pot he had started earlier. He strode back over and slid into the booth across from her. He seemed to own the space. He seemed like the type of man who owned the moment wherever he was, for that matter.

"So, tell me, Gavin, what is it that people in Perfect do for a living?"

"This used to be a coal mining town. The mines closed down about ten years ago leaving a lot of people without jobs. Some people drive to the next town for work. There's a factory there. Others just run small businesses here in town. We're in the process right now of opening an enrichment center. We're hoping to attract people from all over the country. It would open up good jobs that would be close by."

"An enrichment center? Tell me about it."

Gavin leaned back in his seat and raised his eyes up, looking beyond Morgan in thought. "We would like to open a facility that would be a haven for the body, mind, and spirit. In one sense, it would be a spa with massages and mud bathes. For the mind, we would have self-improvement seminars going on and practical programs offered for people who want to change their lives."

"And for the spirit?"

Gavin made eye contact with her again. "I believe when you are physically and mentally at peace, then the spirit will follow."

"Some people would say when your spirit is at peace then your physical and mental state will follow."

"I can't deny the truth in that."

"The enrichment center sounds like just what people are looking for. I hope it's a success."

"That's what I'm hoping."

Morgan studied Gavin with open curiosity. The man seemed so displaced in this small town. Under her gaze, Gavin raised his eyebrows questioningly. "And what do you do, Gavin Antoine? What's your job in this town?"

A sparkle glinted in his eyes. "I'm the mayor."

Had she heard correctly? This man who had gone out of his way to see to her well-being was the town's mayor? It was her turn to raise her eyebrows in surprise.

"It's been a pleasure to meet you, *Mayor* Antoine."

"You know a little about politics, now don't you, Ms. Blake?" He leaned forward in his chair. "If I'm not mistaken, your father is Senator James William Blake of Virginia."

Morgan blinked again. "My stepfather, actually. My biological dad died in an auto accident when I was only a baby. James became my stepdad when I was three, so he's the only dad I've known." She tilted her head. "Not many people make that connection. I certainly don't advertise it."

"Your first book was a political thriller. The depth by which you wrote about the subject made it obvious your knowledge of government was more than average."

"That's a writer's job, to make people believe they know what they're talking about. Anyone writing a political thriller should be able to fool people into believing they've been there." She eyed him curiously. "So, how did you know? How did you know my stepfather was a senator?"

She didn't advertise the fact, mostly because she didn't want people to think she'd gotten to where she was today on his coattails. She preferred fighting for things on her own, a stubborn quality that could frustrate the most patient of people. Like Tyler.

Gavin leaned back in his seat and casually stretched his arm across the back of the booth. "I've been following his career for a few years now. He's quite the senator. We also share the same alma mater."

"You attended Harvard?"

"Quite a few years after your father, but yes. Before I moved here and became mayor, I was a lawyer."

Morgan stored away the new facts. They made Gavin seem all the more interesting and intriguing. And yes, even mysterious.

Gavin tilted his head, his gaze fixed on Morgan. "Your stepfather must be very proud of you."

Morgan shrugged and looked away. "I suppose."

He raised an eyebrow. "Just suppose? That doesn't sound very confident."

The words seemed to get stuck in her throat. "He wanted me to follow in his footsteps. I started law school, but knew it wasn't what I should be doing, so I transferred into a master's program and got a degree in English instead. Unfortunately, anything outside of politics is meaningless to my stepfather. Especially writing novels."

"Surely he must realize novels can be the greatest teachers of all. They teach the person reading without the person ever realizing it."

Morgan straightened, Gavin's words soothing her. "I agree. I like to think that stories were the way Jesus taught and that was how people best learned. Writing novels is just my way of making a small contribution to the world. And besides, I like to write about redemption. Who doesn't need redeeming?"

Gavin's eyes twinkled across the table. "I think you are a remarkable writer, Morgan, and I'm thrilled that you accepted our invitation to come to town. Your visit might just be exactly what the people here need to lift their spirits. The economy has been hard on people across the country, but it's hit this area of Appalachia with a particularly strong force. You're a bright spot in another otherwise glum outlook."

"Thank you." Her cheeks flushed as exhaustion forced her emotions to teeter between embarrassment and appreciation. Glancing at her watch, she saw it was two a.m. already. "I don't suppose the bed and breakfast is open for check-in at this hour, is it?"

"For you they will be. You need your rest if you're going to make it for the book signing tomorrow afternoon." Gavin stood from the booth. "I'll walk you over there."

They left the restaurant and walked in silence down the shadow-filled street, lit by a full moon hanging unobstructed above and scattered streetlights. The night was silent and peaceful, something Morgan welcomed. She felt weary after all that had happened and hoped the walk to the bed and breakfast wouldn't take long.

Despite her weariness, she speculated about the town around her. With its Mayberry-esque setting, she imagined it to be a place where people weren't afraid to keep their doors unlocked at night. Morgan smiled at the thought. Perhaps Perfect was just the town she was looking for.

Morgan's ears perked at a sound behind them. Before she could turn toward the noise, a scratchy voice cut through the air. "Leave before it's too late!"

Morgan's heart raced as she spun around, coming face to face with an old woman with a hunched back. Morgan opened her mouth, trying to find the right words—any words—when the woman hissed, baring stained teeth.

"Get out. Now!"

Chapter Four

"Beatrice, that's no way to treat our guest." Gavin nudged Morgan back a step.

"Don't let them pull you in." The woman leered at Morgan with eyes so wide they looked like they might pop out of socket at any minute. "You'll never get out."

"Pull me into what?" Morgan blinked, trying to understand and to ease the fear that had begun squeezing her heart.

"That's enough." Gavin dropped his arm from her shoulders and took a protective step between the women. "Beatrice, we can't have you scaring away every visitor we have here. I'm going to have to call Sheriff Lowe if you don't behave."

The woman waved a finger at Gavin like an unskilled swordsman going to battle. "You're the one who doesn't behave, Mayor. I was here long before you came in with your fancy clothes and high talk."

"Beatrice," Gavin warned. He raised his chin like a stern father might.

The old woman looked at Morgan again, her sagging eyes full of fire and eerily wide despite the flaps of skin surrounding them. "Don't say I didn't warn you." Spittle flew through the air as she spewed out the words before turning to hobble away.

38

Morgan let out the breath she'd held and turned toward Gavin. "What was that about?"

He sighed, his gaze following Beatrice as she shuffled away. "She's a little crazy in the head. She thinks we're all taking over the town with modern conveniences and it's going to eventually kill us. She doesn't believe in cars or electricity. People say she lost it when her husband died ten years ago."

Morgan's shoulders relaxed. "Poor lady. That's kind of sad."

Gavin nodded. "It is sad. We've tried to help her, but she won't let us."

"Does she really try to scare away all your visitors?"

Gavin nodded and pointed up to a shack perched above Perfect. "Her house overlooks the town, so she can tell whenever something is going on or when someone new is here. I think she's appointed herself guardian. I feel quite terrible for her really, but she won't let anyone help her."

As they continued to walk toward the bed and breakfast, Morgan tried to put the kooky old lady out of her mind by gathering in as much of her surroundings as the dark would allow. Her gaze fixed on a beautiful Victorian home that rested on the corner. The huge wrap-around porch probably held a swing in its dark recesses—another throwback to a gentler time. A warm light by the front door seemed to flicker like a candle. Hanging baskets, full of colorful mums, hung evenly on both sides, warmly greeting visitors.

"Is that where we're going?"

Gavin flashed a grin. "It sure is. The town's one and only bed and breakfast. Unfortunately, it doesn't get used quite as much as we would like. Maybe that will turn around one day. Needless to say, you'll be the only one staying here during your visit. We want to respect your privacy."

"You didn't have to do that, but thank you. I appreciate the effort."

Gavin walked up the wooden steps and knocked on the door. A moment later the curtain at the top of the door fluttered, a partial face peeking through.

The door opened, revealing a twenty-something pulling her robe more tightly around herself. "Mayor Antoine. What brings you here at this hour?"

"Lindsey, I'm sorry to disturb you, but this is Morgan Blake. Morgan, this is Lindsey."

"It's a pleasure to meet you, Ms. Blake." The tousled blond opened the screen door and extended her hand. "Come on in."

Morgan stepped inside, followed by Gavin. As soon as she entered, she noticed the pleasant scent of cinnamon potpourri. The homey aroma made her want to crawl into a warm bed and forget about her troubles.

"I'm sure our guest is exhausted, so let's skip the pleasantries," Gavin said.

Lindsey stifled a yawn. "Why don't you let me show you to your room? I have everything all ready and waiting for you there, including some homemade cookies I baked this afternoon. I hope you like chocolate chip. They're my daughter's favorite."

"That sounds great. Delicious." Morgan turned to Gavin. "Thank you again. I don't know what I would have done without you tonight."

Gavin smiled, still appearing fresh and well put together. Morgan reached for her hair and pushed a piece behind her ear, conscious of her disheveled state. *I, on the other hand, must look like a mess.*

"It's been my pleasure. I hope to see more of you while you're here."

The idea seemed strangely comforting to Morgan. "That would be nice."

They exchanged goodnights before Morgan turned to follow Lindsey up the ornate wooden stairway. "No suitcases?" the hostess asked.

Morgan had forgotten about her car, which was still parked at the Sheriff's Office. It was too late to retrieve her luggage now. "I'll get them in the morning."

"I'm sure Lindsey has something you could borrow. Right Lindsey?" Gavin stood nonchalantly at the bottom of the stairs, his hands lounging in his pockets.

"Of course!" Lindsey ran a hand through her hair and her eyes widened—a little too self-consciously, perhaps. "I should have suggested that myself. My brain feels fried half of the time. I apologize."

"No need for apologies. I appreciate the offer."

Lindsey led her to a room nestled at the end of the hallway and flicked on the light. Stepping inside, Morgan noted the high, four-poster bed, a love seat situated in the corner and an adjoining private bath. "It's perfect."

Lindsey smiled. "I'll leave some pajamas outside of your door for you. Good to have you in town. We're all just thrilled that you accepted our invitation."

"I'm glad to be here." Morgan smiled, tried to reassure her hostess that she wasn't fussy.

After Lindsey slipped out, Morgan picked up a cookie to nibble on. She plopped down on the loveseat, closed her eyes and tried to calm her racing thoughts. Just when she'd begun to relax this evening, Beatrice had appeared and stirred up her anxiety again.

A woman who thought modern conveniences were taking over the planet. Morgan chuckled as the absurdity of the situation washed over her. Maybe the woman was right. As much as Morgan hated using her GPS, she couldn't argue.

Speaking of modern conveniences, she had to call Tyler. Leaning on one elbow, she grabbed her purse and pulled out her cell phone. She resisted the urge to throw it across the room when she saw there was still no signal.

She sighed, wondering for a moment why nothing seemed to be going as planned so far. She'd told Tyler she would call. Now he was going to worry because worrying about her was what Tyler did best. Morgan smiled at the thought. Tyler cared about her. There was no doubt about that. It was too bad that she'd rather suffer Chinese water torture than to ever date someone in law enforcement again. Tyler understood that. He'd never once indicated that he wanted anything more than friendship.

Perhaps Morgan could use Lindsey's phone.

42

She opened her door, stepped over the folded white nightgown that Lindsey had left there, and crept downstairs, careful not to wake anyone. Lowering her foot to the last step, she spotted Gavin and Lindsey whispering in the entryway. As her foot made contact with the riser, a loud creak sounded. Gavin and Lindsey snapped their heads in her direction.

"Sorry to interrupt, but could I use your phone? My cell phone is out of range here."

Lindsey looked at the phone on the wall behind her, a hand going to her exposed throat. Morgan admired her modesty. "I hate to tell you this, but all the lines running into town are down. We had a bad storm about two nights ago and lightning hit the main line that leads into Perfect."

Morgan rubbed the back of her neck as she processed the information. "So, there are no phones I can use anywhere?"

"I'm afraid not."

"They should be up sometime tomorrow," Gavin said.

Morgan frowned. Giving them a brief thanks, she went back upstairs, wondering if there were any angles she'd missed. But with her cell phone out of range and the phone lines down, there was nothing else she could do.

She pictured Tyler looking at the clock, wondering why she hadn't called. He was a patient person. But he also knew if Morgan said she would call, that she would unless something happened. She sighed, deciding to let it go.

Instead, she pulled the covers back. Her bones felt as if they could melt into the soft down duvet. Within minutes, she was out.

***

A noise awoke Morgan. She tried to pull herself from sleep, but her groggy mind drifted between a half-conscious, half-asleep state. The line between reality and dreams sucked her under, making her feel like a drowning woman desperately reaching for the surface, for air. If only she could fully awake …

She jolted up in bed.

Morgan looked around the room, chills creeping up and down her spine. She wiped the sweat on her forehead, evidence of the horrible nightmare she'd been having. The man's face had been pressed up against her windshield and again he'd only said one thing—help.

Helping him was the one thing she couldn't do. She couldn't help someone she couldn't find.

Morgan ran a hand through her hair as the room came into focus. The bed and breakfast, she remembered, her heart rate slowing. The room was still insanely dark, absent of even a streetlight outside. Hadn't there been streetlights outside when she went to bed? With everything that had happened, she couldn't even remember.

Rubbing her eyes with one hand, she reached for the alarm clock with the other. 5:20.

She fell back into the pillow, praying for sleep to come again, but her senses were on full alert and her grogginess gone.

Then she heard it—a moan.

Throwing her feet to the floor, she tiptoed to the door. Whatever the muted sound was, it was coming from somewhere inside the dark house.

She cracked the door open.

Eerie silence slithered inside. Maybe she was just hearing things. Maybe it was still the nightmare playing out in her subconscious.

She waited, gripping the doorknob like a scared child holding a mother's hand, but heard nothing. Just as she was about to close the door, she heard another moan, followed by what was clearly the phrase, "Help me!"

Chapter Five

Chills went up Morgan's spine again. The thought of going out into that pitch-black hallway made her throat go dry. But what if someone needed help?

Slowly pulling the door open, she stepped into darkness so deep it swallowed her. Reluctantly, she let go of the door. As soon as her grasp left the metal, terror rippled through her.

The moans stopped.

She wanted to run back into her room, to forget about this. But she couldn't. Reaching for the wall to guide her, Morgan tiptoed to the stairs and took them one by one, her pace slow so she could listen for another moan.

Skipping the creaky stair at the bottom, her feet touched the hardwood floor. Her eyes slowly adjusted to the darkness and her gaze roamed the room. There was no one in sight.

"Morgan?"

She gasped. Her hand went to the stair railing and she stepped back. A loud creak caused her to gasp again.

Lindsey stepped from the shadows in the hallway. "I didn't mean to frighten you."

Morgan let out the breath she'd been holding in. This was the second time in twenty-four hours she'd jumped at a seemingly harmless woman. She was beginning to feel paranoid. "I thought I heard someone."

"I was afraid you might get worried." Lindsey pulled her housecoat around her. "My husband Rick sometimes yells in his sleep. The nightmares started after he got home from Operation Enduring Freedom in Afghanistan, and they've just never seemed to go away."

Morgan's shoulders sagged with relief. "I'm so glad it's nothing more than a nightmare. I thought someone might be hurt."

Lindsey smiled. "Everyone's fine. Go back to sleep."

Feeling more at ease, Morgan crawled back in bed, vowing to awake early, so she could talk with the sheriff and see what he found out about the man she hit.

Although she didn't awake until noon, she didn't complain. Sleep felt good. Crawling out of bed, she put on the jeans and white sweater she'd worn the day before. When she opened her bedroom door, she almost stumbled over her luggage, which rested there, along with her car keys.

Grateful someone was looking out for her, she hauled her luggage into the room and started a shower. An hour later, she emerged wearing a brown skirt and a crème button-up shirt.

She had an hour before the book signing was supposed to begin. Taking the steps by two, she went downstairs. As she passed the dining room, she saw Lindsey eating lunch with a man Morgan assumed was Rick and a girl who looked to be about eight years old.

"Good afternoon." Lindsey glanced up from the meal. "Let me introduce you to my family."

Morgan tucked a stray hair behind her ear and smiled as she approached them.

"This is my husband Rick." Lindsey pointed to the tall, lean man beside her. He nodded her way, the lines on his face tight and serious.

Morgan's gaze wandered to the little girl. "And this must be your daughter." The girl seated at the table was the spitting image of her mother.

The girl grinned. "I'm Amber."

"Nice to meet you," Morgan said. The smell of food reminded her of the meager supper she'd had last night, but she ignored it. She didn't have time for food at the moment. "I'm heading over to the bookstore to see if there's anything I can do before the signing begins."

"Bonnie's place is right down the street," Lindsey said. "You shouldn't have any trouble finding it."

"Thanks," Morgan said. "By the way, who brought my luggage in?"

"Sheriff Lowe brought it by a couple of hours ago. It appears you left your keys in the car."

Now that she mentioned it, Morgan didn't remember taking the keys from the ignition in her haste to find help. "I'll have to thank him for that. By the way, are the phone lines back up yet?"

Lindsey shook her head. "Sorry. They're still down."

Morgan bit back her disappointment. "Got it. I'll see you later on this evening."

"We'll be by at the book signing, so we'll see you then."

Morgan's eyes roamed over the town as she walked to Bonnie's. Last night in the darkness, she hadn't been able to take everything in. But now, with the sun hanging high in the sky, Morgan was ready to soak in the picturesque mountain town.

The buildings reminded Morgan of a gingerbread village with their gabled roofs and large windows and cottage-like details. The sidewalks were cobblestone and the streetlights the old-fashioned type with a lantern-like light atop a thick black pole. Perfect seemed like quite the unexpected treasure and not what Morgan pictured a former coal-mining town to be.

Looking in the distance, Morgan noted the slate-like clouds waiting on the horizon. There would be a storm here by the day's end. She hoped that Sheriff Lowe had kept true to his word and searched for the missing man again this morning. If not, any evidence might be washed away when the rain came.

Morgan hurried down the street, passing a gift store, a post office, a bakery, and a lawyer's office. Finally she reached *Bonnie's Bookstore*. As she stepped inside, Morgan spotted a redheaded woman reading behind the counter. The woman was so absorbed with the book that she didn't even hear the door open.

Morgan cleared her throat. "You must be Bonnie."

The woman dropped the hardback. Her face lit up in delight when she spotted Morgan.

"Morgan Blake! I'm so glad you could make it. I can't tell you how much this means to a small town like Perfect to have someone like you take the time out to come. We've just been looking forward to your visit like nobody's business." She rounded the counter and stood beside Morgan, talking a mile a minute. "You've been the talk of the town. And that you would come all the way out here for us… we're simply flattered."

"It's good to be here. Really. And I'm the one who's flattered by all of this attention."

The woman's hand flew through the air, simultaneous to a squeal. "Aren't you sweet? Successful and humble. I love that combination." She meandered over to a table adorned with Morgan's books. "Now, I have everything set up for the book signing. We've been advertising this all week, so we expect to have a good turnout. Also, Mayor Antoine suggested we have a social tonight in your honor. Nothing too fancy. Would that be all right? I realize it's kind of last minute."

"That would be nice actually. Very kind of you." It would be nice to get to know the people around here a little better. Morgan's gaze fell on the phone next to the cash register. "By the way, is your phone working?"

Bonnie shook her head, her beehive hairdo not moving an inch. "All the phones in town are down. That would be the one disadvantage to being so secluded out here. Well, that and not having a shopping mall close by."

"Just checking." Morgan not only wanted to call Tyler, but she also wanted to call the sheriff to see if he'd found anything new. "Is there anything I can do to help you get ready?"

Bonnie shook her head. "We just have to wait for the people to arrive. Should start pouring in here in about thirty minutes or so."

"In that case, I'm going to run down to the sheriff's office for a moment. I promise I'll be back in thirty minutes for the book signing."

Bonnie's eyes widened and she leaned closer. "Is everything okay, Ms. Blake? I'd hate to think something's happened that might tarnish your stay here in this town."

Morgan wished she could bottle this woman's enthusiasm. "Don't worry about it, Bonnie. I just have to check on something."

Leaving the bookstore, Morgan hurried down the street. When she walked inside the sheriff's office, one of the deputies directed her to the sheriff. She walked down the hallway and knocked at his door.

"Come in."

She pushed open the door and stepped inside a messy office. It fit Sheriff Lowe—unkempt and overstuffed.

The sheriff looked up from stacks of paperwork and gave a curt nod. He moved his toothpick from one side of his mouth to another, not missing a chew. The action almost reminded Morgan of a baby with a pacifier.

"Ms. Blake. I was just thinking of you."

"Did you find anything this morning? I've been anxious to get some resolution to this whole fiasco."

"Not a thing." He drug in a deep breath as he leaned back in his chair. "Ms. Blake, I'm not saying the accident didn't happen like you said it did, but there ain't a lick of evidence to prove it. Not even any skid marks. Yes, there was some underbrush that was trampled down around the scene, but that could have been caused by a wild animal or even one of my men last night. The tracks didn't lead anywhere, and this man is nowhere to be found."

"So what now?" Morgan asked.

He leaned back in his chair. "You ask me, I wouldn't worry your pretty little head over it. We'll keep our eyes open for anything that might come up. Otherwise, we really don't have a case."

Morgan stared at him in disbelief. "Sheriff, I really don't think dismissing this case is plausible when you could have an injured young man lying in the woods somewhere needing help."

"My guess is that he's not as hurt as you think he might be. If he could run away and make it far enough that we can't find him, then I'd guess he might only have a broken bone or two. Nothing more serious than that, though."

Morgan leaned over the sheriff's desk. "You don't understand, Sheriff. The only thing this man said to me was 'help.' I don't intend to give up on him."

Sheriff Lowe glanced down at his desk and then back up at Morgan. "We'll search again to see if anything turns up. Don't get your hopes raised, though. I doubt we'll find anything."

"Thank you." Morgan stepped away from his desk. With a nod to Sheriff Lowe, she headed back for the book signing. For now, she would have to be content knowing they would search again.

Chapter Six

"Tyler? Are you with me, man?"

Tyler turned his gaze from the window of his cruiser and snapped his attention to his partner, Craig. "Sorry. I guess I'm in another world."

"Thinking about your lady friend?"

Tyler smiled. Craig sometimes knew what he was thinking before he did. They'd been partners for a few months and could read each other pretty well already, an important quality to have while working together.

"Morgan," Tyler said. "Her name is Morgan."

"Yeah, Morgan. She's one fine looking lady." He raised his dark eyebrows in curiosity. "What's going on?"

Tyler shook his head. "It's a long story."

"We have time."

Tyler wasn't normally one to share his personal life with coworkers, but Craig seemed interested and Tyler could use someone to talk with. "Basically, she took this trip to West Virginia, promised she would call when she got there, and she didn't. I'm concerned."

"It's written all over your face, my man." Craig grinned, the white of his teeth a bright contrast against his dark skin. "You've got it bad for her."

Tyler looked out the window again. "I can't argue with you there."

Tyler sighed. "You're too new on the force to know about everything that happened. Braden O'Sullivan was her fiancé."

"Braden O'Sullivan? The officer who was killed in that drug deal gone bad? Your former partner?"

"That's the one."

"Sounds tragic."

"It gets worse. He died three days before their wedding."

"Ouch."

"Yeah, ouch is right. An understatement, actually."

"Does she know how you feel about her?"

Tyler shook his head. "No. How I feel about her doesn't matter. I don't think she's over Braden's death yet and, even if she was, she's made it clear she never wants to date a cop again. She wants someone with a 'safe' profession."

"She could change her mind."

"I don't want to put her through that again." Tyler shook his head, remembering her grief in the months after Braden's death. "No, they had something special. I just have to figure out how to get over Morgan."

"Hanging around with her all the time certainly doesn't seem like it would help."

"You're probably right. I just…"

"His death wasn't your fault."

"I always think about the 'if onlys'…"

"What happened, happened. And it could happen to any of us. The guilt lies only in the hands of that drug dealer who pulled the trigger. No one else."

He'd heard that a million times before. But Braden had been his best friend, and he'd been on the verge of something great—marriage. All of that had been taken away with one pull of the trigger by a thug who'd now be spending the rest of his life in jail.

Braden and Tyler had met the first day at police academy. They were opposites in so many ways. Five years later, they became partners, and during that time they'd developed the true bond of friendship. They'd been as close as brothers.

Tyler still remembered the day when Braden told him about Morgan.

"She's the total package. Beautiful, smart. Her stepdad is a U.S. Senator. Oh yeah, and she's published. Wrote some suspense novel that's being optioned by a movie company now. You're going to love her."

Tyler had his doubts. He'd expected someone who thought she was better than everyone else. That would fit the description of all of Braden's prior girlfriends, at least.

But when Tyler met Morgan, she was nothing like he expected. Sure, she was bright and intelligent and beautiful. But she was also humble and sweet and kind. She never name dropped. She didn't even bring up her writing unless asked and, when she did talk about it, her voice tinged with passion.

Braden was right—Tyler was going to love her.

He'd actually found himself falling *in* love with her.

—

56

Not that he would have ever acted on those feelings, especially not with his best friend dating her. Instead, he avoided her whenever possible—probably to the point of being rude. But Morgan Blake had intrigued him from the start. Honestly, he loved his best friend, but Braden seemed mismatched with Morgan. The two took life at a different pace and had nearly nothing in common. He supposed that's why opposites attracted, though.

Then Morgan's novel was actually made into a movie. Fame like that might have changed some people. Not Morgan. She just blushed when people talked about it, and made her media appearances seem like a visit to the grocery store.

Tyler's cell phone rang. He glanced at Craig before answering, the silent question of whether or not it was Morgan hanging in the air. No such luck.

"We've got a homicide over on Atlantic. We need you there right away."

"We're on our way," Tyler said.

Lunch would have to wait until later, as would his worries about Morgan.

***

Morgan rounded the corner from the sheriff's office and stopped in her tracks. A line wound down the street. People holding books and pens chatted with each other, their conversations as easy as a summer breeze.

Was this the line for the book signing? If so, it appeared everyone in town had turned out. There had to be at least 200 people out here. She'd done book signings before, but never one like this.

Morgan continued walking. As she approached the line, several people called out hellos and reached out to shake her hand. She followed the winding crowd. They led down the sidewalk to Bonnie's.

Morgan pushed through the door and into the dimly-lit store. Bonnie was pacing by a table where Morgan's picture was displayed.

"Oh, you're back! I was getting worried!" The redhead grabbed Morgan's arm and directed her to a leather chair. "Everything's ready. We were just waiting for you."

Morgan flashed a smile, trying to ease the woman's anxiety. "I'll take over from here, then."

Bonnie opened the door and the chatter from the outside muffled the country music whining through the overhead.

For the next two hours people poured into the store. Morgan tried to answer all their questions and make small talk. Faces she recognized came through, including the sheriff and his deputies, and Lindsey and Rick. Donna from the café came by and introduced herself. So far she hadn't seen Gavin. Her heart sunk at the realization.

Why does it matter, Morgan? You'll be leaving town tomorrow, anyway.

But when the line dwindled and she spotted Gavin at the end, her heart lifted. Morgan watched as Gavin made it a point to let others go before him, so he could be last. When it was his turn, he proudly set her book before her.

"Would you please sign my book?" His eyes twinkled.

She grinned. "With pleasure."

Writing a quick message in the cover, she snapped it shut and handed it to him. Gavin's eyes sparkled, almost with mischief, and he opened it.

"To my Good Samaritan, thank you for your kindness. I hope to repay you some day for all your help," he read aloud. He closed the book and peered at her, his blue eyes still sparkling. "Perhaps you could repay me by allowing me to escort you this evening to the reception at City Hall."

"I'd love to."

"Bonnie, do you need Ms. Blake any longer or can I take her off of your hands?" Gavin called.

"She's all yours, Mayor." Bonnie straightened the remaining books stacked on Morgan's table. "Thanks again, Ms. Blake. I've done more sales today with you here than I've done all year. This was just the bump I needed."

Morgan and Gavin stepped outside, a devilish wind whipping around them. The ominous sky looked like it would burst any minute. They would have to hurry to make it inside before the storm hit.

"Did you sleep well?" Gavin strolled beside her, not the least bit ruffled by the weather.

Morgan crossed her arms to ward away the chill. "Besides one nightmare about John Doe I slept fine."

"I imagine you may be having those nightmares for a while. You're handling this situation with strength. I admire that."

Morgan shook her head. "I don't feel very strong."

"It's obvious in your determination to find him. It shows strength of character."

"Some people might call that stubbornness," she said lightly.

"Well, I'm sorry your arrival here happened the way it did. I do hope that won't change your opinion of our town."

"I'll give it a fair chance." She grinned.

As a drop of rain splattered Morgan's arm, Gavin motioned for a car parked across the street. The Rolls Royce pulled up beside them a moment later. A Rolls Royce? Really?

Gavin opened the door for her. "Your chariot awaits, my lady."

As soon as they both climbed in and Gavin shut the door, the sky exploded. The rain pounded on the roof, drowning out every sound except the swish of the wipers.

"That was close," Morgan muttered.

Moments later they pulled to a stop. Gavin hopped out and opened an umbrella. As Morgan stepped from the car, she paused and stared at City Hall through the watery downpour. It certainly wasn't what she expected. It was at least five stories high and the outside walls around it were reflective mirrors, which gave the building an elegant, expensive look. The massive structure seemed out of place, but then again a lot of things seemed misplaced here.

"You seem surprised," Gavin said.

"Things around here haven't ceased to amaze me yet. I certainly didn't expect this, though."

"Expecting a small, rundown building?"

Morgan blushed, realizing she was caught. "This just seems like the Taj Mahal."

"It's part of my vision for Perfect. There's a lot to be said about the packaging of a product, a person, or even a town. If we here in Perfect want people to be drawn here for an enrichment center one day then we need to package ourselves for success. City Hall was just the first part of that plan."

Morgan nodded. "I see. That makes sense. Although, with the down economy and dire job situation, it's just surprising. Forgive me if I'm being too blunt."

"Not at all. I appreciate your honesty. To tell you the truth, I've been financing most of the improvements throughout the town."

She swiveled her head toward him. "You paid for this?"

He chuckled. "I wouldn't have mentioned it if you hadn't asked, but, yes, I did. I did mention to you that I used to have a law firm. We won some pretty extraordinary cases and made quite a bit of cash. I invested most of that money, and now I'm using some of those funds to help this town."

"Why? Why Perfect? Why not stay in Boston?"

"I stumbled upon this town a few years ago. I was going skiing and got lost, truth be known. I was so taken by the people here, and by their stories of what this town used to be like in its heyday. I'd always had this dream of opening a place for people to come to for refreshment—a spa for the total person. Moving here just seemed right."

"And you went from simply moving here to being mayor by...?"

"I bought a couple of businesses and hired some people to help with various projects I envisioned. I don't want to brag, Morgan, but I guess I brought hope to the people here. They encouraged me to run for office, and I couldn't resist. I never saw a career in politics. I always thought of myself as more of an attorney and entrepreneur. But sometimes God has different plans."

Morgan smiled. "Yes, He does. I can't argue that point."

Gavin held out a hand and nodded toward City Hall. "Shall we?"

"Let's."

Morgan slipped her hand in his and together they stepped inside a building most metropolitans would envy. A huge fountain greeted them at the entryway. They rounded the fountain and stepped through one of the doorways into a reception hall. Black, silver, and white balloons decorated the room along with a skillfully arranged buffet. Morgan's stomach grumbled again, protesting her neglect of food as enticing aromas filled her senses.

Applause sounded when she walked into the room. For the next hour she talked with people from the town, grabbing bites to eat in between. Gavin was a faithful escort, staying by her side and joining in to her conversations. She didn't miss the hopeful smiles a few people sent to Gavin. Smiles that seemed to say, "This could be a good match."

Gavin did intrigue her, as well as send a zap of electricity through her every time he offered his hand. But the fact that she felt so initially drawn to him scared her. She liked taking things slow—at least, when it came to relationships she did.

She'd dated plenty. Well, she'd dated plenty before she met Braden. Since his death, her ideal for a relationship had been turned upside down. Sometimes she didn't feel like she knew herself very well anymore, even.

In the middle of a conversation about one of her books, Gavin grasped her elbow. "We need to get you home. You had a late night last night and need your rest."

Morgan could have hugged him for noticing her exhaustion. She politely excused herself and allowed Gavin to lead her away from the reception. As soon as the sound of everyone closed away with the door behind them, relief filled her.

"Thank you." Her gaze fluttered to Gavin's in appreciation. "My late night is catching up with me."

"It's quite understandable."

The rain still pounded outside as they approached the doors. Gavin found his umbrella and pushed it open as he waited at the door for her. She joined him under the waterproof fabric and together they dashed toward his car. Gavin's arm slipped around her waist as they squeezed together in order to stay dry.

Heat rose on Morgan's cheeks as she realized how much she enjoyed the closeness to Gavin. Everything about him screamed intrigue and excitement.

With relief, they reached the car and Morgan ducked inside. Gavin quickly followed suit. Once the door was closed behind them, they both sighed from the exhilaration of their quick dash. As Morgan ran her fingers through her hair, her gaze caught with Gavin's. Lightning flashed behind him, followed by the rumble of thunder.

Suddenly, she was all too aware of his spicy cologne and the slight stubble that was beginning to form across his chin. Her instant attraction to this man scared her. And fascinated her. There was no need to dwell on that, though. She wasn't ready for a relationship. Sometimes, it didn't feel like she would ever be.

"It's quite the storm we're having tonight." Gavin maintained eye contact, the action connecting them like electricity.

"Yes, it is." Morgan generally was at ease with conversations, but at the moment she felt speechless. There was something about the way Gavin looked at her that put her at a loss for words.

Just as the ride began, the car halted. Morgan looked away and swallowed deeply, again grateful for the distraction. She almost wished Gavin wouldn't walk her to the door, so she could avoid his tantalizing gaze and try to make sense of her tangled emotions. She knew arguing would be futile, though. Gavin already expanded the umbrella and waited in the rain.

Drawing in a deep breath, Morgan stepped from the car. Her nearness to Gavin again sent shivers down her spine. Finally their heels clunked on the wooden porch and the porch light invaded the romantic feel of the stormy night.

Gavin's gaze again caught hers and she purposefully looked away.

He reached for Morgan's chin and gently turned her head toward him. "Will you be staying any longer now that the book signing is over?"

Why was she letting this man have this affect on her? It was ridiculous. Gathering her wits, she said, "I was planning on looking for a nice little town where I could stay for a few days and start writing my new book."

"I know of a nice little town that would be thrilled to have you stay a few days…"

She grinned and nodded toward Main Street. "I didn't have to look very far."

"I'm glad." His eyes pulled her into that trance-like state again. "Would you join me for dinner tomorrow night?"

A battle raged inside of her. *You have no reason not to, Morgan. One day you will need to start dating again.* Still, she hesitated. "I should write," she mumbled.

Gavin tilted his head. "You have to eat sometime, now don't you? Why not do it in the company of a new friend?"

———

65

His words convinced her. Gavin was a friend. That was all. There was no reason to feel jittery and like a schoolgirl with a crush. "Dinner. With a new friend. Why not?"

A smile lit up his face. "Wonderful. I'll come by to pick you up around six thirty."

"I'll see you then."

He brought her hand to his lips and kissed it softly. "Goodnight, Ms. Blake."

Morgan's throat felt dry as a grin stretched across her face. "Goodnight, Gavin."

Chapter Seven

The next morning, Morgan took a sip of hot chocolate and leaned her elbow onto the kitchen table. Lindsey dried a muffin pan at the sink, and Morgan observed the woman. She had a slight build that almost made her appear girlish. Her quiet, subdued demeanor made Morgan wonder if people often tried to walk on her. Her husband also seemed quiet, but in a harsh, almost brooding way.

Morgan realized she was staring and cleared her throat. "This is quite a town, Lindsey. I was amazed last night at how friendly everyone was."

Lindsey finished drying the muffin pan and slipped it inside a cabinet. "Oh, yes. Everyone is always well-behaved. It's such a safe little town to live in."

A picture of the man Morgan hit flashed through her mind and caused a sick feeling to form in her gut. *Until I came along, it was safe*. She pushed away the rest of her muffin before she could finish. Her appetite was gone.

How could she have been enjoying herself last night, worrying about her romantic feelings toward a man, while someone could very well be dying in the woods somewhere? Was she really that self-absorbed?

"Do you want to talk about it?" Lindsey pulled out a chair across from her, a steaming mug in her hands.

Morgan touched the rim of the porcelain plate where her muffin laid discarded. "I'm just concerned about the man I hit. I worry that the police aren't doing enough."

Lindsey patted her hand. "Just let the police do their job. You worry about yours. I think you mentioned you had a book to write?"

Morgan nodded. "You're right. I have to trust Sheriff Lowe to handle things." She cast out the picture of the man pressed against her windshield. Sitting at the table and worrying would do her no good. "Speaking of writing, I should probably get back to work. I'm becoming a great procrastinator."

"You go on upstairs and work all day if you need to. I'll try not to let Amber up there to bother you."

Morgan smiled. The little girl had seemed to latch onto her. Not that Morgan minded.

Back upstairs Morgan sat in front of her laptop computer, rereading the work she had done in the early morning hours. It wasn't her best, she decided, but it was a start.

As she calculated her next plot twist, her thoughts drifted to Tyler. She grinned as she pictured him. His squared jaw-line and brown eyes beckoned her. She thought of his chestnut-colored hair, slightly tousled after he'd been outside.

Tyler was a good man. He'd been such a good friend to her since Braden died.

She still marveled over how opposite the two best friends were. Braden had been the life of the party. She liked to say he always had two things on hand: a joke or a strong opinion. Sometimes both. He was brash, but passionate; stubborn, but loyal; quick-tempered, but justice-seeking. He liked to live big and often spent beyond his means just to embrace the moment. His hair almost looked red when the sun hit those strands, but most considered him a brunette with a lean but scrappy build.

Tyler, on the other hand, looked all-American. Tall with broad shoulders. He was steady, dependable and kind. He'd bought the first house he could afford when he was just a rookie cop, and instead of moving out of the blue-collar neighborhood at the first opportunity, he'd decided to fix the place up himself. He'd done a wonderful job with it. He liked time with his family more than parties; having a few close friends to a large circle of acquaintances.

Morgan knew that part of the reason he'd been around so much was because he felt guilty. Tyler felt like he should have been able to stop the thug who shot Braden. She'd tried to persuade him to find no fault in himself. He was still hanging around, so she assumed her pep talks hadn't worked.

She'd stopped complaining, too. She had to admit that she enjoyed his company. He stopped by after work with his dog, Columbo, and they took walks on the beach. He invited her to family outings where Morgan always stayed entertained while watching him wrestle with his nephews or swing his nieces. He'd been a bright spot in an otherwise drab season of her life.

You're holding him back.

She twitched. Where had that thought come from?

Was she being selfish, enjoying his company when she should encourage him to be free? Guilt pounded at her heart. He probably wouldn't leave her side... not until Morgan found someone to take Braden's place, at least.

The few guys she'd been out with after Braden's death just didn't interest her. She'd known right away and hadn't wanted to lead any of them on. Everyone else thought it was because she still mourned Braden. But she didn't. She'd dealt with that grief, and now she struggled to find new footing.

Maybe tonight's dinner with Gavin would be a good thing... on more than one level.

***

At lunchtime, Morgan decided to walk to the sheriff's office to see if there were any new developments. It felt good to stretch her legs. The walk alone made her feel better, more at peace. She prayed as she went that there would be some kind of new development.

There was no one at the front desk at the office, so Morgan wandered down the hallway until she came to Sheriff Lowe's office. She was about to knock when a conversation caught her ear.

"All the evidence is gone. There's no proof of anything. I told her not to worry about it." Pause. "She's a writer. You know how they have big imaginations." Pause. "No, I didn't say she imagined it, but …" Pause. "All right. Got it."

Did the sheriff think this was all her imagination? Irritation tensed her neck muscles. He had a lot of nerve. She did not imagine hitting that man, no matter what anyone thought.

Without bothering to knock, she pushed the door open. The sheriff's mouth gaped open, but only for a second. "I gotta go. I'll talk to you later." As soon as the phone was on the cradle, he smiled up at Morgan. "Ms. Blake, what can I do for you today?"

"Sheriff." The warmth left her voice. There were a few good qualities she'd learned from her stepfather. Being assertive was one of them. Two bad the negatives he'd shown her outweighed the positives. "I trust you're still searching for the man I hit."

"Sent my men out this morning. I'm sorry to say this, but they didn't find anything. As far as I'm concerned the case is closed." He raised his palms in resignation, his ruddy complexion filling with color.

"As far as you're concerned I just made all of this up. Isn't that correct?"

Sheriff Lowe's cheeks filled with color. "No, ma'am. We just can't find any evidence the accident did happen."

"I didn't make it up, Sheriff."

He shifted in his chair again. "I know we've been through this before, but I think the best thing at this point would be for you to just forget it happened. There's nothing further we can do."

There had to be some evidence somewhere. But with no skid marks and no tracks through the woods, what else was there? Somewhere, Morgan felt confident, there was some proof.

She closed her eyes and replayed the scene in her mind.

The dent in her car hood. That would be proof.

"I have some evidence for you." She opened her eyes and fixed her gaze on Sheriff Lowe.

He raised his eyebrows. "Take me to it then."

The sheriff drove them to where her car was parked across the street from the bed and breakfast. Thick silence permeated the air between them as they rode, and Morgan found herself still fuming over the conversation she overheard.

Let him doubt me all he wants. I have the proof right here.

As soon as the car stopped, Morgan sprinted to her Miata. She ran her hands across the hood to find the indention. When she didn't feel the uneven surface, she leaned over the body of the car

Her gaze slid over the smooth metal. The hood was like new, with no dent in sight.

Morgan's stomach twisted.

Maybe she was losing her mind, after all.

Chapter Eight

Morgan was still mulling over the disappearance of the dent on her car hood when Gavin arrived to pick her up at six o'clock. Lindsey called upstairs, letting her know he arrived, and Morgan hurried down. When Gavin came into view, Morgan was pleased to see him dressed casually in khakis and a polo shirt.

His approving gaze swept over her. "You look beautiful."

She'd worn a simple black dress that fell just above her knees, accessorizing it with a pearl necklace and earrings. Add a cardigan, and she'd look like a politician's wife, she mused.

She smiled, determined to forget about the day's frustrations and enjoy the evening. Talking things over with a new friend would be just the right cure for her headache. And if Tyler wasn't here, maybe Gavin would work just as well.

"Ready?" He offered his arm.

She rested her hand in its crook. "Starving."

He chuckled. "I was hoping you might be looking forward to spending some time with me, but if it's just the food I'll understand."

Despite her weariness, she smiled. "It's the food and the company."

Once in his chauffer-driven car, she settled back for the ride. She'd half-expected him to take her to Donna's again, as that seemed to be the only restaurant in town, but as the ride lengthened, she guessed otherwise.

Gavin turned in the seat beside her and fully faced her. "You look exhausted."

She let out a half-sigh, half-laugh. How much did she share with this man? She hardly knew him. But he seemed logical and reasonable. In the brief time she'd known him, he'd seemed like friend material. "It's been another one of those days."

"Promise me that tonight you'll forget about your problems and just enjoy yourself."

"If only I could promise that." If only that were possible, for that matter. Her gaze flickered back up. "There's so much on my mind that I'm slightly distracted. I apologize in advance for that."

"Well, I can't have you spending your entire visit here in our town with the weight of the world on your shoulders. What can I do to relieve some of the worries weighing on your mind?"

"If I start talking about what's on my mind, I'll consume the entire conversation this evening."

He offered a gentle smile. "I wouldn't mind."

They pulled to a stop in front of a sprawling brick house. Morgan stared at the structure. This town would never cease to amaze her.

Gavin followed her gaze. "I thought I'd have someone prepare something for us here, if that's all right with you."

"That's fine," she mumbled absently.

She continued to stare at the house before her. She knew Gavin had said that he'd developed quite a financial portfolio thanks to his time as a lawyer, but wow. The town itself had already surprised her enough that she should have been prepared for this.

The chauffeur hurried around to let her out. She stepped out of the car and felt dwarfed by the giant house before her. She noted the similarities between this structure and her parent's house in Virginia. Both were regal and conservative, showcasing eight large columns and uncountable steps leading to the front door.

Gavin appeared beside her. "What do you think?"

"It's beautiful."

"Glad you like it." He placed his hand on the small of her back and led her inside.

The rich overtones inside were spectacular. The colors were dark and the wood a deep mahogany. The furniture was lush and original artwork hung on the walls.

"Let's go have a seat in the study." He led her into a room on their right. "I'm going to go check on dinner. Can I bring you something to drink?"

"Water, please."

As he walked away Morgan roamed the room, pausing at the blazing gas fireplace. She stayed there until her chills subsided. Still, just the enormity of the house left her feeling cold and small. She felt the same way at her parent's home, she supposed. That's probably why she'd chosen to purchase a cottage on a less frequented beach back in Virginia.

She perused the bookcases surrounding her. They were filled to capacity. She ran her finger along one shelf, reading the titles aloud. There were some classics and several books on philosophy.

"See any favorites?" Gavin entered the room with two goblets of water. He sat them down on a coffee table in front of the leather couch.

"Several actually. I take it you like to read."

"Absolutely."

They discussed their favorite books until Chef Fanelli announced it was time to eat. They followed him to a cozy table for two in the dining room, complete with candles and a linen tablecloth. Gavin pulled back her chair for her to be seated.

"Something smells wonderful." She eyed the Italian dish before her. Chicken, peppers, and mushrooms rested atop linguini and were covered in a cream sauce. Salad and fresh bread waited on the side.

Morgan couldn't help but think about how different this was than her last dinner with Tyler. They'd tried to cook rack of lamb with risotto. The meat had burned and the risotto turned out like a paste. They'd doubled over with laughter at their pathetic failure. Finally, they'd ordered Chinese take out. Morgan smiled at the memory.

Gavin offered grace before they began to eat. After eating a few bites of her meal, Morgan brought up the incident that had occurred today with the sheriff. Gavin listened intently as she spoke.

He seemed to be processing all the information. As a counselor might, he nodded and focused his full attention on what she was saying. She could certainly see why the people of the town thought so much about Gavin. He had charisma and confidence, two key ingredients for leadership. And when he spoke there was something very convincing about his words.

"I don't know what happened to the dent. But it was there. I saw it." She looked at him with confusion in her eyes. "Do you believe me?"

He leaned forward and took her hand. "Morgan, you are one of the most intelligent women I have ever met. I have no doubt you are telling the truth."

Relief flooded through her. "I wish I could be that sure. I'm starting to question what I saw myself." She studied his sculpted face a moment. "What do you think happened to the dent then? Is there something I'm missing here?"

"I wish I could tell you." He leaned back and looked into the distance. "But I don't know. I don't even have any good ideas. The law is my specialty, not mechanics, I'm afraid."

She released the breath she held, ruffling her hair in the process. "The sheriff thinks it's my imagination. I don't know what to think anymore."

"The sheriff doesn't know what he's talking about then."

Morgan's heart lifted some. Maybe she wasn't losing it after all. Gavin seemed to think her story had merit.

"Did you… hire Sheriff Lowe?" She tried to tread carefully with the question.

Gavin seemed to pick up on exactly what she was implying because a grin spread across his face. "He was sheriff when I arrived here. He's not the brightest bulb around, but the people seem to like him. Besides, we don't have any crime here so his position is something close to a formality. Occasionally, he does catch someone for speeding, I suppose."

"Do you trust him?"

Gavin paused. "Trust him? To uphold the law, you mean?"

Morgan shrugged. "I suppose."

"Of course. He may be backward thinking at times, but at his core he's a good man."

"Right. Maybe I'm overthinking things." Even as she said the words, she didn't believe them.

He wiped his mouth with a linen napkin. "What else has been on your mind? I've got all night, and I only charge a nominal fee for my listening ear." He grinned again.

"You've been a saint listening to me as much as you have. We should really talk about something normal. Something like… the weather? Football? The rising price of gas?"

He chuckled. "Talking about you is much more interesting. I love the people in town, but none of them are as well-read or cultured as you. It's refreshing to speak with someone with whom I can relate."

"I'm afraid some of the people in this town have me up on a pedestal. I'm really just normal. Nothing special."

"I'd have to disagree."

Morgan felt the heat on her cheeks and looked away, which sent Gavin laughing.

"I didn't mean to embarrass you."

She nodded, not willing to deny his claim. "You're charming. I'll give you that."

"Charm is deceptive. I speak the truth."

Morgan shook her head and raised her finger. "There you go again..."

"Forgive me for enjoying your company so much."

"Fine, if I have to, then you're forgiven." She grinned before leaning back in her chair and crossing her arms. "I know this question is so cliché, but why aren't you married? You're the type of man that..."

He quirked a brow. "That what?" His voice held a teasing tone.

Great, now she had to finish that ill-timed statement. "That women want. Happy now?"

"Happiest I've been in years. The simple answer is that I haven't found the right one. So, I'll turn the question back to you. Why aren't you married? You're the type of woman that..."

Morgan resisted the urge to slap his forearm. No, that would seem too much like flirting. They were already making enough headway in that area. She wiped her mouth, trying to form her thoughts into words. "Well, I was engaged actually."

"What happened?"

"Three days before our wedding, my fiancé was killed during an undercover drug bust."

Gavin blinked and pulled his head back. "What a tragedy."

Morgan nodded. "It was a shock, to say the least. The news rocked my world. I just keep trusting God that He works everything for a purpose."

"Even death?"

She nodded. "Even death. I think He can take the pain in our lives and turn it into something beautiful if we let Him. I'm not quite there yet, though."

"How long has it been?"

"Two years."

"Grief takes time."

She tapped her finger on the table. Where did the conversation go after dropping a bombshell like that? "So…"

Chef Fanelli appeared with two slices of cheesecake, both drizzled with chocolate, and broke the moment— thankfully. "Are you ready for dessert, sir?"

"We'll take it on the patio," Gavin instructed. He stood from the table. "If you'll follow me."

They walked through the open glass patio doors on to a balcony. The view from the expansive stone-paved enclave was spectacular as it overlooked dark mountains sprinkled with tiny lights from the town below. Eating dessert here was the perfect ending to the evening.

"You like it?" Gavin stood close beside her, close enough that her skin seemed to dance. He followed her gaze and looked over the town. He appeared to be more of a king looking over his domain. This man had power. An unusual amount of power. And wealth.

"It's breathtaking. Where can I get a view like this?" She couldn't pull her eyes away.

"This is one of my most treasured spots. It's the perfect place for an early morning read. The sun rises right over those hills in brilliant colors. It leaves me speechless sometimes."

Putting his hand on her back he led her to one of the cushioned chairs around a glass top table. "Have a seat."

Chef Fanelli placed their dessert before them and they dug in. Mid-bite, Gavin paused, his eyes glimmering with curiosity. He lowered his fork to the plate and leaned back.

"Have you found what you're looking for in life yet, Ms. Blake?"

She took a slow bite of cheesecake, chewing on his question. "I think so."

"So, you've arrived, would you say?"

Morgan shook her head. "I don't believe living life is about arriving. I think it's about the journey. That's the beauty of it, the adventure."

He nodded, admiration in his eyes. "Wise answer."

"Why do you ask?" She tilted her head, surprisingly wary of where this conversation might go.

"You're someone who appears to have it all. You have success, wealth, good looks. I just wondered if there was anything else out there for you to desire."

"One might ask you the same question then. Is there something more in life you want?"

He glanced at the table before answering. "There's always more to want. Life isn't fun anymore if you don't have dreams."

"And what's your dream? The enrichment center?"

Half of his lip curled. "Yes, that's part of my dream. I just want to show people hope. When I first arrived in town, this place seemed like hope had moved out along with the jobs." He finished his dessert, stood and offered his hand.

Tentatively, she slipped her hand into his and stood. They walked to the edge of the patio and looked over the town. "Have you started building yet?"

"We broke ground a few months ago. I'd like to have everything up and running by next summer. We'll have to invite you to the grand opening."

"That sounds nice."

"You are very beautiful, Morgan." He turned toward her.

Her heart raced as he stepped closer. But instead of enjoying the moment, her thoughts turned to Tyler. She scolded herself. Gavin was fascinating. Chemistry sparked between them, drawing her to him. Why did she feel so drawn to this man? She'd been around plenty of other handsome and charismatic men without feeling like a schoolgirl with a crush. But there was something different about Gavin…

Gavin's hands went around her waist and he pulled her toward him. His eyes again captivated hers. Morgan sucked in a deep breath.

He was going to kiss her. And if she didn't rein in her emotions, she might let him. Or maybe she should let him? If there was one thing Braden's death had taught her, it was that she wasn't very good at relationships.

"Mr. Antoine, you have a phone call." Chef Fanelli stepped out the patio doors.

A look of annoyance crossed Gavin's face as he pulled away from her. "One moment." He glided inside and took the cordless phone from the chef.

Morgan let out the breath she held. Thank goodness for the interruption. She had to start thinking straight. Why did this man seem to cast a spell on her?

Morgan watched him pace back and forth inside, an animated conversation taking place. Then, as if a light bulb went on in her head, she realized the obvious.

The phones were working again. In fact, Sheriff Lowe had been using one earlier, but she'd been so distracted by everything else she didn't realize it at the time.

She'd be able to call Tyler.

Gavin hung up the phone and walked back toward her. Before he even closed the patio door, she asked if she could use his phone.

"Of course. Why don't you go into my study, so you can have some privacy?"

Did she imagine it or did annoyance flicker through his gaze? As soon as the emotion materialized, it was gone. Of course, Gavin seemed like the kind of man who was used to getting what he wanted. Having their evening interrupted just might be enough to annoy him.

"I'd appreciate that. Thank you." She took the phone from the counter and walked into the cozy room. Closing the door behind her, she dialed Tyler's number. She paced as she waited for him to answer.

Her gaze roamed the library again as the phone rang. She paused by some pictures on the opposite side of the room. She squinted up at them before sucking in a breath.

The buildings in the photos were mostly shacks, most tinged with a black dust. Coal, perhaps? Potholes scarred the roads, and liter cluttered the street.

And there, on one of the signs. Donna's.

These were pictures of Perfect.

Is this what the town had looked like before Gavin got here? If so, he really had turned things around.

"Hello?"

Warmth filled her upon hearing Tyler's voice. "Hey. It's me."

"Morgan?"

A grin tugged at her lips. "Expecting someone else?"

"No, but I was expecting you sooner. Are you okay?"

She curled half of her lip dubiously at his question, remembering her trip so far. "It's been interesting, but I'm okay. The phone lines were all down in the town I'm staying in so I couldn't call you sooner."

"Where *are* you staying?"

"You'll never believe me, but I'm in a town called Perfect, West Virginia."

"That's actually the name of a town?"

She paced the room, her gaze scanning her surroundings. "It sure is."

"So, where are you now? Are the phones back up?"

The concern in his voice made her heart do an unwilling flip. "I'm having dinner with the mayor. And yes, the phones are back up. Thank goodness."

"Dinner with the mayor? A little town like that, the people are probably enamored with your celebrity. At least the mayor and his family are, huh?"

She cringed. "Well, the mayor perhaps is. He doesn't actually have a family." She bit her lip, imagining how it probably sounded. Why did she feel so hesitant to say that? She and Tyler were just friends. She never wanted to date a cop again, not after what happened with Braden.

Silence passed until Tyler spoke again. "It's 9:30 at night. Isn't that a little late?"

"Depends on who you ask, I suppose."

He paused, but only for a moment. "Morgan, I'm worried about you. I have a bad feeling. I was battling the temptation to go out and search for you. At the very least I was going to start calling local hospitals to see if you'd been in an accident."

"Not everything in life demands an investigation, Detective. Besides, don't you think you're overreacting a little?"

"I've learned over the years to trust my instincts, Morgan."

"I appreciate that you watch out for me. But there's no need to worry. I'll be okay." He seemed appoint himself her guardian after Braden died.

Maybe this wouldn't be the best time to bring up the incident that happened on the way here. She couldn't stop herself, though. It would gnaw at her until she spilled it.

She licked her lips. "I need your advice about something that happened. Promise me you won't overreact, though."

Morgan could imagine Tyler putting his hands on his hips and narrowing his eyes. He was so overprotective sometimes. She had to admit that she liked that quality about him, most of the time, at least.

"I'll do my best."

She opened her mouth and heard a click. "Tyler?"

There was no answer.

"Tyler? Are you there?"

When there was still no response, she pressed the talk button. Silence answered.

What had just happened?

Chapter Nine

"You've got to be kidding me," Morgan muttered, staring at the phone in her hands. She'd really wanted to talk more, but at least Tyler knew she was safe now. It was better than nothing.

She found Gavin waiting for her on the patio, again staring out over his domain. Her presence seemed to startle him, but delight quickly overcame his surprise. He turned and grasped her hands.

"No one's worrying about you now?" he asked.

She wobbled her head back and forth like a pendulum and shrugged. "The phone line went dead."

He pointed in the distance to where the sky lit up. "An approaching storm. Out here in the country our phone connections aren't very good in the first place, but when there's any excuse for them to get worse, they do."

Morgan felt a cool breeze from the impending storm and shivered. "There sure have been a lot of storms lately."

"It's that season." He stroked her arm, an unreadable emotion in his eyes. "Perhaps I should get you back to the bed and breakfast before the storm arrives."

Her heart sunk in disappointment. She had enjoyed her time here, talking with Gavin. But he was right, she should get back. "Perhaps that's a wise idea."

They walked through the house, to the front door. "If it's okay, I'm going to let my driver take you back. Some unexpected business came up. That was my City Manager who called. We have to smooth out some rough edges on one of the new projects we're working on."

"I understand. Thank you for a lovely evening."

"Thank you for the lovely company." He kissed her cheek, his spicy cologne again filling her. She could drink in that scent all day and not complain. His hands grasped her arms for a moment, as if he didn't want to let go, and his eyes probed deeply into hers. "You are beautiful, Morgan. I hope you'll have dinner with me again before you leave."

Without thinking, the words escaped, "I'd love to."

He kissed her cheek again before walking her to the car. As she pulled away, Gavin waved at the door. Seconds later, the sky broke with an all out autumn thunderstorm.

***

The next morning, Morgan pulled her knees to her chest in an effort to ward off the chilly morning air. Last night's storm had raged on for over two hours with vicious lightning and rumbling thunder. The air had a new brittleness to it today.

Morgan lounged on the porch swing, lazily swaying back and forth. Her favorite jeans and an oversized sweater were perfect for the cool day. Around her, birds chirped their early morning songs in harmony with nature and a misty fog gently draped itself around the mountains.

Despite her peaceful surroundings, her heart was at unrest. Gavin Antoine was making quite an impression on her and guilt gnawed at her. Was she ready for another relationship? Was Gavin even offering? And why couldn't she stop thinking about Tyler?

Her thoughts danced from one tangent to another and then back again. As they turned again to Gavin, she mentally scolded herself. She only had three more days until she was to leave and here she was wondering if she and the mayor could have a future.

She already knew the answer to that question—no. Getting to know him better with the intention of something other than friendship was not a possibility. Even if she was attracted to him, she had other tasks to give her attention to.

A creak at the front door pulled her out of her thoughts. Her gaze darted across the porch to where Amber pressed her face into the screen door, her eyes fixed on Morgan. Morgan smiled.

"You're pretty," Amber said in a sing-song voice.

Morgan leaned into the swing, casting aside her heavy thoughts for a moment. "You know what, Amber? So are you."

"I know."

Morgan's heart warmed and she patted the space on the bench beside her. "Want to come out here and sit with me?"

Without hesitation, Amber threw open the screen door and skipped to the swing. She plopped down beside Morgan and grinned, her face beaming.

"Why do you look so happy?" Morgan ruffled Amber's hair.

"Are you going to marry Mayor Antoine and move to Perfect?"

The question startled Morgan and it took everything inside her to keep her mouth from gaping open. Amber's big, blue, expectant eyes told her she'd have to handle the question delicately.

"Where did you get that idea, sweetheart? I've only just met the mayor."

"You had dinner with him yesterday. And everyone keeps saying that Mayor Antoine is waiting for just the right person to come along. We all love Mayor Antoine here."

Morgan tilted her head, trying to soften her response. "Amber, I have a life back in Virginia Beach. I'm not going to be able to stay here in Perfect forever."

Amber's smile disappeared. "You don't like it here?"

"Of course I like it here. But I'm just here for a visit. Mayor Antoine is a wonderful man, but he's just a friend, nothing more." No matter how fascinating Morgan found him...

"I didn't like Perfect when we first moved here." Amber's eyes lost some of their glow, but her voice was still animated. "But now I like it a lot."

Morgan remembered Lindsey telling her she was born and raised in Perfect. Maybe she'd misunderstood.

No sooner had she thought of Lindsey than did the woman step out the door, hands on hips. "Amber, are you bothering Morgan?"

Amber shook her head. "She invited me to swing."

Lindsey sent Morgan a questioning glance.

"We're just having an early morning chat," Morgan said.

She still didn't seem convinced. "Amber, why don't you come back inside and give Ms. Blake some time by herself?"

Amber nodded and shuffled toward her mother. Before the screen door closed behind them, Lindsey mouthed, "Sorry."

"Lindsey," Morgan called.

The woman paused.

Morgan nodded toward her arm. "That's a bad bruise you've got there. Everything okay?"

Lindsey glanced at the mark, and something flashed in her eyes. Panic? Fear? "I'm just clumsy. Bumped into the wall earlier. I feel rather silly about the whole thing, actually."

"Sorry to bring it up then."

Lindsey nodded and slipped inside. Morgan's mind remained on the bruise, though. Had she really bumped into a wall? Why did Morgan always think there was more to the story than there actually was? An overactive imagination, she supposed. It's what made her a good writer.

But she knew her imagination wasn't always working overtime. She'd seen abused women. She knew the fear in their eyes. She knew the control their spouses tried to exert over them.

Was Rick abusing Lindsey? Morgan shook her head. She didn't know. She'd keep her eyes open for more signs.

And then what?

Then she'd tried to help. It might seem brash or nosy, but Morgan couldn't stand by and see someone suffering at the hands of another human being. For now, she would observe.

The smell of something sweet floated outside. Morgan abandoned the porch swing and stepped back into the cozy home just as Lindsey took a pan of banana nut muffins from the oven. She seemed just like the homemaker type.

And also like her self-esteem was low enough that some man might take advantage of it.

"Would you like some hot chocolate or coffee?" Lindsey offered.

Morgan cleared her throat, trying to brush away her thoughts. "Hot chocolate, please."

Morgan sat at the kitchen table next to Amber and waited for the muffins to cool while Lindsey busied herself making Morgan's drink. A moment later, Lindsey placed a steaming mug in front of Morgan and went back to washing dishes. As Morgan listened to the chatter around her, Morgan's eyelids grew heavy.

Perhaps everything that had happened was beginning to take its toll.

Lindsey squinted at Morgan. "Are you feeling okay? You look a little pale."

Now that she mentioned it, Morgan didn't feel the greatest. Aside from her heavy eyelids, her head was starting to throb. Maybe it was the change in her diet that caused her to feel so sleepy lately? The fresh mountain air? Or maybe it was even the warm milk Lindsey used to make her hot chocolate. Didn't warm milk put people to sleep?

"I think I'm going to take a little nap here in a moment. I'm feeling a little tired." She finished her hot chocolate and muffin, making small talk with Lindsey and Amber.

"Amber, you need to finish your lessons," Lindsey muttered.

"Lessons? Are you homeschooled?"

Amber nodded. "Everyone is."

Morgan blanched. "Everyone?"

Lindsey stepped forward, drying a pan a little too hard, Morgan thought. "We don't have a school up and running here, and the bus ride to the closest county school would take about forty-five minutes. So most of us just homeschool. It's easier that way."

"Makes sense." Morgan's gaze roamed the house a moment. "Where's Rick, by the way? Is he out of town?"

Lindsey nodded, sitting across from her and sipping her coffee. "He travels a lot with his job. He left this morning."

"What does he do?"

"He teaches workshops called Seminars for Life. It keeps him gone a lot, but he loves his job."

Morgan soaked in the new information. What Amber had told her this morning about moving to Perfect still bothered her. "So, you said you've always lived in Perfect?"

Lindsey again nodded. "Born and raised. Both Rick and I."

Morgan wondered why Amber had said she didn't like it when she first moved here. For all Morgan knew Amber could have been adopted. No, she decided. She looked too much like her mother to be adopted. It probably wasn't important anyway. Morgan had just been curious.

Amber looked up from her homework. "The answer is twenty-three. That's my mom's age."

"Oh, Amber, Morgan doesn't want to know that information. Keep doing that multiplication."

"You're only twenty-three?" Morgan had known the woman looked young, but she thought she just had good genes.

Lindsey blushed. "You caught me. I … started young, you could say."

They talked a few more minutes and then Morgan excused herself. She went upstairs and fell into the comfort of her bed, letting sleep invade her.

***

Morgan awoke from her nap two hours later. Her heart was racing, her breathing heavy. She had another dream about John Doe. The accident had occurred all over again. Except this time she realized something new. John Doe hadn't just been standing in the street. He'd been running from something. The crazed look in his eyes, the fear that was there—it was from more than just being hit. He was scared of something long before he and Morgan collided.

The thought hung heavy in Morgan's mind. She couldn't escape the haunting image. But the more she thought about her new theory, the more sense it made. The dream conjured up something in her subconscious, something real and useful.

She tossed the theory back and forth in her mind. Who or what would the man have been running from? A wild animal? A delusion? A person?

She shook her head at the possibility. The sheriff was right—she did have quite an imagination sometimes. Why would someone have been chasing him? And wouldn't she have seen them if they were? It didn't make sense.

Wandering into the bathroom, she splashed some water on her face. Staying in bed all day wasn't acceptable. She had to get something done.

After towel drying her face, she went downstairs. She would get something to eat and then try to work on her book some more. On her way out, Morgan came across Lindsey sitting at the kitchen table reading a book.

"Are you feeling any better?" Lindsey closed the book. Morgan sat across from her, her limbs still feeling heavy.

"I don't know." Morgan ran her fingers through her hair. She stopped midway through, leaving her hand atop her head. "I just …"

Lindsey leaned toward Morgan, waiting for her to continue.

"I keep thinking of the man I hit." Morgan told her about her dream and about her theory. When she was finished she lifted her head. "Do you think I'm crazy?"

Lindsey shook her head. "No, I don't."

"Thank you. Sometimes I just feel like I'm losing my mind."

"You've had a rough couple of days. But I would suggest forgetting about that man you hit."

"Why's that?"

"Because I can see you're worrying about it. We shouldn't worry about things that are out of our control."

"We just have to distinguish what's in our control and what's not, I suppose." Morgan tilted her head, a new thought coming to mind. If she could find out what happened to the dent in her car, maybe she could find out what happened to the man she hit. "Are there any mechanics in town?"

"Just one. Tony Gavaro. He has a shop a couple of blocks from here." She knit her brows together. "Everything okay with your car?"

"I'm just thinking about the dent on my hood after I hit the man. I know it was there. The only thing I can think of is it was smoothed out and repaired between the time I arrived and the next morning."

"But why would someone do that?"

Morgan hesitated. "I have no idea."

"If it would make you feel better, why don't you go ask him? It can't hurt. Though I do suspect if he was guilty he wouldn't be quick to admit it."

"In which case it would be futile to even ask." Morgan sighed.

"Have you asked Sheriff Lowe about it?"

"Sheriff Lowe thinks I have an overactive imagination. I'm not going to get any help from him."

Lindsey patted her hand. "Maybe you should take a couple days just to rest. You've been through a lot."

Morgan shook her head. "I have to know what happened."

Lindsey caught her gaze. "Be careful, Morgan."

A knock at the door prevented further conversation. Lindsey rose from the table and went to the front door. Sheriff Lowe's voice sounded from the kitchen.

"Is Ms. Blake here?"

Morgan heard footsteps as Lindsey led him into the kitchen. He took of his hat and greeted Morgan with a curt nod. "I just came by to check on how you're doing this morning."

Morgan blinked in surprise. "I'm doing okay. I appreciate the inquiry."

"If there's anything I can do for you while you're here—"

Gavin must have had a talk with the town's sheriff, Morgan guessed. "Will do."

He drew in a deep breath and cracked a forced smile. Placing his hat atop his head, he nodded. "I'll be talking to you later then."

As Lindsey walked him to the door, Morgan's gaze fell on the book that Lindsey left on the table. The author was a man by the name of Joshua A. Sutherland. Where had Morgan heard of him before?

She started reaching for the book when Lindsey walked back into the room. "That was nice of the sheriff to stop by and check on you, wasn't it?" Lindsey snatched the book from the table. "Well, I have to do some laundry. Don't work too hard."

When Lindsey left, Morgan sunk back into the chair and dropped her head in her hands.

What was she going to do now? She had no story ideas, no clue what happened to the man she hit, and her heart felt like a tangled mess, torn between the urge for self-protection and the allure of risking again.

This vacation was not working out as she planned.

Chapter Ten

The basketball hit Tyler in the chest, pulling him out of his thought vortex and back to the game at hand.

"You're gone again. Here, but not here." Craig grabbed the ball and bounced it a few times on the cracked court. The autumn sun was beginning to sink in the sky and, any moment now, the normal crew would be dismissed from middle school and join them on the inner-city basketball court. "What's going on?"

Tyler shrugged as Craig passed him the ball. "Just stuff."

Craig paused and gave him a knowing look. "Look, why don't you just surprise your lady friend by showing up for a visit?"

"Because then it will seem like I'm smothering her. No woman wants to be smothered. And I don't want to be overbearing. She deserves better than that." He made a shot and watched the ball circle the rim before sliding through the basketball hoop.

"What is it that's got you all up in arms about her being away?"

Tyler shook his head as Craig snatched the basketball from the ground and took a shot. "I can't pinpoint it exactly. There's just something off about this whole trip."

"She must have done plenty of book signings. What's the big deal?"

Tyler grabbed the ball this time. "They didn't even give her the name of the town when they sent her directions."

"Oversight?"

"Maybe." He dribbled the ball some more. "The whole situation just reminds me of one of those scams. You know those people from other countries who send you emails saying they've got a large sum of money they want to give you if you'll just send your bank account number?"

"You said she's a smart lady. She wouldn't fall for something like that."

"Yeah, you're probably right. She's smart. But she's got a big heart that sometimes clouds her judgment."

"What kind of scam could there possibly be that would drag her out to West Virginia?"

Tyler paused, spinning the ball in his hands. "Her stepfather is a U.S. Senator. Do you know how many people could use her for a darker purpose? Her stepfather has made some pretty controversial votes lately. There have been some threats."

"True that." Craig stopped, hands on his hips and listened.

"And she's had a couple of 'fans' who were over the top. One tried to break into her house even, and she had to get a restraining order against him. Her celebrity—even though she would never call herself famous—also makes her a target."

"That it does."

Tyler shook his head, studying the cracks in the asphalt at his feet for a moment before raising his gaze to meet Craig's. "I've got to let it go, don't I?"

His friend shrugged, snatched the ball from Tyler and made a free throw. "That depends. You've got good instincts. You could do something totally out of character."

"Nice shot." Tyler grabbed the ball again. "What's that?"

"Show up in West Virginia, and tell her how you feel. How you really feel. Take the risk. Make your surprise visit seem all warm and fuzzy, not overprotective. Women love that kind of stuff."

"I'll think about it." He tossed the ball back to Craig, just as two of the kids from the mentoring program they were a part of approached. Tyler put those thoughts aside for a moment. Right now, he had another task to focus on.

***

Morgan resisted the urge to bang her head against the wall at Donna's as she faced another unsuccessful morning of working on her book. Only that haunting first line remained.

I remember the day darkness slithered into our home.

God, I feel like You've given me that line, You've told me I should use it, and I have no idea what to do with it.

My power is made perfect in weakness.

Why had that verse come to mind? Was her inability to write supposed to somehow bring glory to God? She shook her head before turning her attention back to her computer.

Her other books had been politically charged. That opening line… well, she supposed she could twist it into something that would work. She just didn't know what. Nor did she know what was blocking the creative process in her life.

She sighed, ready to close her laptop and give up. But, before she could do that, her finger brushed a key on her computer, and her picture folder popped open. She leaned forward and studied the image on the screen. A smile stretched across her face. The photo was of her and Tyler at the beach. She'd had his family over for his thirtieth birthday, and they'd had a party in her back yard—which just happened to be on the shores of the Atlantic Ocean.

In the picture, Morgan laughed so hard that she doubled over after Tyler's sister poured ice water down his shirt. Tyler had decided to avenge Morgan, who he'd said was guilty by association, by wrapping his arms around her until the icy coolness that had statured his shirt crept through to hers also.

She chuckled as she remembered the moment. The photo was a great one, taken by Tyler's sister Harley who was studying photography at a local college. She'd used the party to practice her skills. This picture captured Morgan and Tyler's relationship perfectly. The sun hit their hair at just the right angle and the crashing waves in the background completed the professional look of the photo.

She touched Tyler's picture on the screen. She missed him. She really did. This was one of the first times they'd been away from each other since their friendship started, and until this moment she didn't realize exactly how attached she'd become.

She flipped through the rest of the pictures. More pictures of her and Tyler together, grins across their faces in each one. One of them with lemonade in their hands, the liquid sparkling in the sunlight. Another of the two playing volleyball in the sand—Tyler's expression much more intense than hers. More photos followed. Splashing at the water's edge. Tyler wrestling with his nephews. Sucking up his pride for long enough to let his niece do his fingernails. His dog, Columbo, tackling him to the ground in a game of Frisbee.

Her smile slipped as the next photo signaled the start of a new photo album.

Braden.

In the early photos, their smiles were broad. As the photos went on, neither of their grins seemed as bright.

Things had changed between them. They were opposites, and the initial qualities that had attracted to them to each other eventually—and sadly—caused them to clash.

Morgan thought about how different her life would have turned out if she and Braden had gotten married. It wasn't that she was thankful for his death—not in the least. But she did know that it was better that they hadn't married. She just wished he hadn't had to die. She would never wish death on anyone.

Things had started to change after the movie deal went through. Suddenly Morgan had a lot of attention. She did a string of media appearances and magazine interviews and even attended the movie premiere in Hollywood. She went from starving artist to being financially secure. Maybe that would be hard for any man to take. She'd just turned in her third book when he'd been killed in the line of duty.

People thought it was her grief that stopped her from writing, but it wasn't. She didn't know what it was. Should she force words out? Should she write something she wasn't proud of just to prove she could still write? She didn't know.

"Are you sure I can't get you something else to eat?" Donna appeared with a pitcher of water.

Morgan nodded. "I'm fine. Just working on my next book."

"Must be a real tear-jerker. You look like you've been crying."

Morgan wiped under her eyes. Sure enough, there was moisture there. She sat up straighter, suddenly feeling silly. "Yeah, a bit of a tearjerker, you could say." She inhaled deeply. "You know what? I think I will have some of that pie you've been talking about."

Donna smiled. "My husband won Best Pie in New Jersey with that recipe, you know."

"New Jersey? Did you live there?"

She raised her plump shoulders and sighed. "It seems like another life ago. My husband and I owned a bakery there. The recession hit us hard, though, and we had to close the place down. Broke my heart. Broke Bill's soul."

"Donna, I thought you'd always lived in Perfect. That this restaurant had been dying, and Gavin bought it from you and helped bring it back to life?" Morgan had even seen the pictures of the town a decade ago, and Donna's had been there, clear as day.

Donna shifted. "This restaurant was dying, and Gavin did buy it. It was after he bought it that we moved here, though."

Morgan shifted in the booth. "How'd you end up in Perfect?"

"We met Gavin at a seminar he was doing on financial security. He told us about Perfect, and we fell in love. For the first time in a long time, we felt hope. We felt like we'd found a place where our children could have a better life, where we could get away from the craziness of the city and live life at a slower pace."

"But the restaurant was already named Donna's…"

A sheepish grin played on the woman's lips. "You caught me. My real name is Dawn, last name was Arnold. Dawn A. It just seemed close enough for me. We wanted to keep things authentic, you know."

No, she didn't know. And how strange was that? Hadn't Gavin clearly said he'd bought the restaurant from Donna? Or maybe he'd said Dawn, and Morgan assumed it was short for Donna. "I've been calling you Donna. You should have corrected me."

"I would never correct you." She waved a hand in the air like a prim and proper southern belle might ruffle her handkerchief.

"Why in the world not?"

"Because you're Morgan Blake."

"I'm nothing special, Dawn." Why did this town seem to have her on a pedestal? She wasn't used to the attention.

The woman waved her hand in the air. "Oh, and so humble too! Let me get you that pie. Aren't you just the sweetest thing! No wonder everyone loves you so much."

Everyone loved her? Morgan shook her head in wonder. Most people didn't recognize her or her name. Not really. It was only if she made a special appearance or did a lecture that people might seem a little star-struck. Being here where everyone knew who she was felt a little strange.

Dawn placed a piece of chocolate pie on the table, grinned broadly, and trotted away, leaving Morgan to stare at her laptop and eat.

After looking at those pictures of Tyler, now she really wanted to talk to him again. This time, she needed to tell him about the man she hit on the way here. She needed his advice and measured wisdom. She could really use one of his bear hugs, too, now that she thought about it.

Why couldn't the phone lines be back up? She'd checked this morning and, sure enough, they were still down. If they weren't fixed by tomorrow, she would drive back out to the interstate and try to find a signal. She had to talk to Tyler.

Lord, I'd like to think you're watching out for me. Could you stop trying to teach me lessons for a moment? Would you just let me catch a break this one time? Please? Let me talk to Tyler.

Morgan wrestled with her thoughts as she ate. By the time she left the restaurant, she was no closer to a solution. She stepped onto the cobblestone sidewalk, tugging her laptop case over her shoulder. The fall air was cool and its breeze pulled at her thoughts, soothing them away from her.

"You should have left when I warned you."

Morgan gasped and spun on her heel. She came face to face with Beatrice. On instinct, Morgan's eyes darted to her surroundings, looking for a way of escape, if it came to that. Several people hovered nearby, eyeing the woman in front of Morgan. Morgan turned back to Beatrice.

The woman pulled a colorful, old shawl around her shoulders and leered at Morgan. "It's too late now. They've got you."

"Who's got me Beatrice?" Morgan narrowed her eyes in curiosity.

"This town, that's who. You should have left when I warned you."

Beatrice's gaze cut through hers. For a moment, Morgan believed the woman actually knew what she was talking about.

"You think they just called you here for a book signing?" She laughed spitefully, a sound that made Morgan's stomach twist into a knot. Her head swung in pity at Morgan. "You should have never come here, girl."

And with those words she turned to walk away, leaving Morgan staring after her in disbelief.

Morgan had the urge to yell after her, though she didn't know what to yell. She wanted to somehow determine the level of this woman's insanity. Instead she stood there, frozen.

She shouldn't have let the words from the crazy old lady get to her. They made no sense. But despite Morgan's logic, she still shuddered.

Back to the bed and breakfast, she told herself. She had to write, despite the other temptations around her. She was determined to stay in for the rest of the evening and do just that, even though her nerves and her curiosity had been pricked.

Chapter Eleven

Tyler hung up the phone and sat back in his desk chair, letting the information he'd just received sink in. Concern and curiosity had driven him to do some research on Perfect, West Virginia. He didn't like what he'd found out.

There were newspaper articles about mysterious disappearances, all happening in the same area of West Virginia near Perfect. A secluded mountain town…what could be dangerous about that? If Tyler had to guess, he'd say drugs. Someone was running some kind of operation out of the area and anyone who threatened to expose it was being killed off. He'd put a call in to a friend with the FBI to see if his theory was true.

Had Morgan been pulled into the middle of it? The thought made his blood boil. As the daughter of a senator, she was already a target. Add to that her wealth and her sweet spirit and Tyler could see the perfect storm brewing.

"Have you heard from your lady friend yet?" Craig asked from his desk beside him at the police station.

"Called two nights ago. Said the phone lines were down in the town she was staying in." Tyler took a sip from his Styrofoam coffee cup. "Get this—the town's name is Perfect."

"Is that what you're looking for on that map on the computer?" He nodded toward the website open on Tyler's desk.

"It's so small I can't even find it."

"Any reason you feel the need to find this town on a map?"

"It's just a feeling I have, really."

"A bad feeling?"

Tyler stared ahead for a moment before nodding. "It may not be the town itself I'm worried about. Morgan was about to tell me something last night when suddenly the phone line went dead. I just keep wondering what it was."

"Did she give you any hints?"

"She said, 'You'll never believe what happened on my way here' and then the line went dead. Not only that, but she called at 9:30 from the mayor's house. She was having dinner with him."

"Do I hear some jealousy in your voice?" When Tyler didn't answer, Craig continued. "You have to remember, man, this is a small town. Having an author like Morgan there had probably stirred up things. I'm sure everyone is giving her a lot of attention."

"You're right." Tyler leaned back in his chair. "I just need to let it go."

Lacing his fingers together in front of him, he steepled his index fingers. He tapped them in a steady rhythm as he ran the possibilities through his mind. Finally, he unclasped his hands and stood.

He was going to West Virginia.

For the next half-hour he took care of business at the office, clearing his leave time and updating Craig on what was going on. Then he hurried home and packed his bags. After dropping Columbo off at his sister's house, he got on the road. A million thoughts raced through his mind. All of them involved Morgan.

The woman had a hold on his heart like no one ever had before. He appreciated their easy friendship, though he longed for more. He knew Morgan's reasoning, though. He knew how Braden's death had affected her. Even knowing that, he still couldn't give up the hope that maybe one day…

As soon as he crossed the West Virginia line he began looking for the exit. Perfect wasn't a town you could find on any map, but Tyler had a vague idea of where it might be from his research.

A few miles later he spotted the exit. He began heading into the mountains. Not much longer until he'd see Morgan. Not much longer.

***

Morgan tried to shake off Beatrice's eerie warning. She strolled down Main Street, trying to enjoy the simplicity of small town life. She'd never experienced a sense of the community as strong as the one here. Her gaze lingered on a poster in the window of Bonnie's Books. The town's fall festival was coming up this weekend. Didn't that sound like fun? Too bad she would probably be gone before then.

Ahead, she spotted Tony's Repair Shop.

Tony.

One of the only people in town who could have fixed the dent on her car hood.

Impulsively, she walked toward the business. When she stepped into the garage, she spotted legs sprawled underneath a car. The smell of oil and sweat mingled inside the small shop. Morgan cleared her throat, and the mechanic rolled out.

Tony was a tall, muscular man with a shaggy mustache and even shaggier sandy-brown hair. She recognized him from the book signing. The man greeted her with a quick smile, wiping his hands on a grimy towel he grabbed from a nearby bench.

"What can I do for you, Ms. Blake?"

"I was wondering if you would mind checking my car for me. I like to have someone look at it before I take long trips, just to check the fluids." It sounded logical, she reasoned.

"Sure, no problem." He rested his hands on his hips as his gaze roamed over his shop. "Do you want to bring it over now for me to look at?"

"Would you mind? I would really appreciate it."

"For a pretty lady like you, it'll be no problem." He winked.

"I'll be right back then."

Grabbing her keys from her pocket, she quickly walked to her car. She jangled the keys as she walked, wondering how to approach the subject. As she started her car, an idea came to her. It would be perfect.

She drove to Tony's and pulled into his garage.

"Pop the hood for me," he asked when she'd parked. She did as he requested and then stepped from the car, tossing him the keys.

"Do your thing. I'll just sit over here and catch up on some reading." She took a place in a chair to the side, only pretending to read the book she grabbed from her car at the last minute. She kept one eye on Tony as he worked.

His head popped out from behind the hood a few minutes later. "Everything looks good. You should be good to go."

"Would you mind starting her up just to make sure she's running right? I keep hearing a clicking sound. It worries me."

He wiped his hands with a stained white rag. "Why don't you start her up? You don't want me in your car with all this grease on me."

Morgan rose and forced a cough. "Actually, if you don't mind, I need to get some water." She coughed again. "Feel free to start it yourself. A little dirt won't hurt my car." Before he could object, she hurried toward the water fountain in the distance.

She leaned down to get some water, but turned her head slightly to watch Tony. Sure enough, the mechanic reached inside her car and opened the door.

He knew that the outside door latch didn't work without even trying.

That could only mean that he'd worked on her car before. It was the only explanation. For some reason, someone in this town was trying to cover something up involving the man she hit. Now Morgan had to find out why.

He started the car and revved the engine. After a few minutes passed, she reappeared, plastering a bright smile across her face. "Sorry about that. How is she sounding?"

"I don't hear anything wrong. Could you be more specific?"

She pulled her lip down in a half-frown. "You know, I don't hear anything either. Maybe it was just my imagination. I've been a little on edge since I arrived in town."

Tony cut the engine and stood. "I heard about the accident. Was wondering how you were taking things."

"I'm still hoping the police will find the man I hit."

Tony's Adam's apple bobbed up and down. "You never know."

Something in his expression made her think he knew a lot more than he let on. But Morgan had a feeling he was just a pawn in this mystery. Judging by his simplistic attitude, he'd simply done what he'd been told—or paid—to do.

"How much do I owe you?"

He waved her off. "Don't worry about it."

"You're sure?" She reached into her purse for some money.

"You know how much trouble I'd get into for doing that? No way."

She stepped closer. "Trouble? Why would you get into trouble?"

Tony cringed. "You're our guest of honor. We're supposed to treat you like royalty. Of course."

She nodded, unsure how to take his words. "That's sweet of you. I would hate to get you in trouble. Thanks, Tony."

She climbed into her car and pulled away. Morgan knew she could have confronted him about the dent, but he wouldn't have told her anything. Besides, that might only put her in danger with whoever was covering up this ordeal.

The important thing was that Morgan felt confident now that someone was hiding something. The question was who and why.

Chapter Twelve

When Morgan pulled into the parking lot beside the bed and breakfast, Gavin was sitting on the porch swing with Amber, the bench lazily gliding back and forth. She grabbed her laptop from the back, swung it over her shoulder, and started toward the front door. As Gavin stood to greet her, Morgan couldn't help but admire his presence. His lean build was only accentuated by his confident poise and charismatic aura. Just seeing him made her heart speed.

"Just thought I'd stop by and say hello. How has your day been?" Gavin's eyes seemed to beam as he spoke with her.

She decided to keep her visit with Tony quiet for now. She still had questions to sort out before she confided in anyone, including Gavin. "I took a much needed nap. How about you?"

"I've had quite a pleasant day myself. Even more pleasant now that I see you." His blue eyes fluttered toward her car. "Take a drive?"

"Just a short one." She leaned against the railing on the porch, trying to control her racing thoughts. She needed some time alone to sort them out, but didn't want to act suspicious. "I had to make sure my car was still running since I haven't driven it all week."

Morgan couldn't be certain, but his eyes seemed to narrow, as if he didn't like her answer. "You're not going to leave us any time soon, are you?"

"Not until the end of the week."

Amber let out a weak cry and scrambled inside. Morgan's heart went out to the little girl and she started to go after her, but Gavin put his hand out.

"She gets easily attached. She'll be all right," he told her, his voice low. "She's just at that phase where she wants attention. And no one wants to see you go. It's fun having a celebrity in town."

"I'm hardly a celebrity."

"To us you are."

"Maybe I won't leave Perfect after all, not with my ego being boosted all the time as it is here." They only saw the side of her they wanted to see. Most people did. If people really knew her, they'd know that she hated politics, she distrusted men, she struggled with her image of God, and she determined her worth based on her success. She tried to use perfection to cover her flaws, but they were always still there, just beneath the surface.

My power is made perfect in weakness. There was that verse again. It seemed to come to mind at the oddest times.

"If you wanted to stay, I wouldn't argue or stop to convince you otherwise." Gavin flashed that winsome grin. "You have time for a walk?"

"Some fresh air would be nice." She put her book down. "Let's go."

"I thought I could show you around town."

"All I've really seen is Main Street so that sounds nice. I'd like to learn more about the area."

Morgan ran her laptop up to her room before meeting Gavin outside. They strolled beside each other past Donna's and Tony's and Bonnie's Books. There was also an attorney's office, a bakery, a grocer and a hardware store. On the corner stood a community church, white, steepled and picture perfect.

Gavin spread his hand to showcase the town. "As you can see, we've got everything we need right here."

Morgan shoved her hands into the pockets of her windbreaker. "It's surprising for a small town. Don't get me wrong—I think this is all great. I wish more small towns could sustain themselves like Perfect. In fact, maybe you should all be a model for towns across the country."

Gavin chuckled. "Not a bad idea. Everyone's looking for a slice of community, aren't they? We have that here."

Morgan liked the thought of that. Where she lived was large and transit with the military presence there. Aside from her involvement with church, she had little sense of community.

Just at the edge of town, nestled in the woods, was an old park. Two picnic shelters, several benches and some playground equipment. A stream trickled by, a rickety looking bridge sprawled over it. Off in the distance was a gazebo, probably beautiful in its day.

Now, it was brown and missing some boards.

"That's the old park. It's the next thing on our list to demolish."

Morgan paused by the gazebo. "I like it just the way it is."

"This old place? It's an eyesore."

"It's got character. I bet the benches and shelters could tell some stories." She ran a finger down the length of the bench. "And look at all of these initials carved here. It's like a history of the town."

"Sentimental, are you?"

She straightened. "I've been called that before."

"I do suppose the park has a charm of its own."

Morgan cast a glance up at him. "But you're still going to redo it, aren't you?"

He smiled and they began walking again. "You already know me too well."

They continued the walking tour, veering in a different direction to a new corner of the town. As they passed the sheriff's office, chills went up Morgan's skin as she remembered her first night here, her panic to find someone to help her. Then Gavin had shown up and somehow everything had worked out.

Except for the man she hit.

"This town is pretty safe, right? Hardly any crime?"

"That's right. Why?"

"I was just thinking how surprising it was that a town of this size has so many sheriff's deputies. It seems a bit like overkill, doesn't it?"

"Well, they have other duties also. They help with some general maintenance of the town. Plus, I think part of the reason we're so safe is because we have a large sheriff's department. When I got here, the area was poor and depressed. Sadly, with those two qualities also comes desperation."

"You've done amazing things here. It takes a lot to amaze me, so I don't say that casually."

He smiled. "I'm glad you're impressed." He extended his hand. Morgan glanced at it a moment before slipping her fingers into his. It had been a long time since she'd strolled hand in hand with anyone.

The road got steeper as they neared the outskirts of town. They walked several feet before they rounded a bend and stopped. Morgan looked at the start of a new building. "The Enrichment Center."

"We're calling it Blue Mountain Lotus."

"Blue Mountain Lotus? It has a nice ring to it."

"Let's go this way a moment." He tugged at her hand, and they walked around the outskirts of the construction toward the woods. "I promise…we're not going far."

She shivered as the forest surrounded them, as the scent of damp earth tingled her senses. The crispness of the leaves and their crunch under her feet brought back memories of staying with her mom and stepdad at their second home up near Smith Mountain Lake. Of course, where they stayed was more of a resort, but still, she'd always thought it was beautiful there. She'd escaped to be by herself and sit by the lake and write, even as a teenager.

Her poor stepdad. He'd wanted an extrovert but instead he'd gotten a by-the-book introvert. Sure, she pushed herself outside of her shell. She had to in order to succeed in public relations. But, at heart, she was an introvert.

Yep, her stepdad had had big expectations for her. She'd never been able to live up. Morgan was too unconventional for him, and the more he pushed her to act one way, the more she'd pushed back with her own ideas. She'd never been fully accepted by him. Not by Braden, either, for that matter.

Was it any wonder that she viewed God as harsh and controlling? The two most important men in her life had been that way. They'd made her feel like she never measured up.

Lord, I want to think You're different. To know You're different. But how?

Mist rose in the distance, and the sound of running water met her ears. They stopped at the rock's edge, and a waterfall tumbled before them. Pristine water fell in a steady stream from a hundred foot cliff above. Water scrambled in a pool underneath them before running down the mountain.

"That's a sight."

"It's called Widow Falls."

She raised an eyebrow. "Widow Falls?"

"The story is that there was a coal mining accident here in the early 1900s. Ten men from the town were killed. Some of the widows suffered such grief that they didn't want to go on with life, so they plunged themselves over this cliff and into the waterfall. Thus it became Widow Falls."

"Chilling name." Morgan shivered even thinking about it.

"I agree. The town has a bit of a tragic background."

She stood a safe distance from the edge but still close enough to feel the mist rising from the cascading water. Despite its morbid past, the majesty of the falls was mesmerizing. "It's beautiful."

"Much like you." Gavin turned toward her.

Shivers went up her spine at his nearness. Was she even ready for a relationship? Yes, she decided. She'd been ready. As long as it was with the right person. Was Gavin the right person?

She never was good at taking risks. And she was way too analytical at times when she was supposed to go with the moment. Like now.

"Morgan?"

She looked up just as Gavin's lips covered hers. Shivers raced up her spine. Or were those chills?

Gavin reminded her of Braden, she realized. Why hadn't she seen in before? But he wasn't Braden. Could she ever get past that?

Gavin pulled back and stroked her face with the back of his fingers. "Am I being too forward?"

"I'm just being cautious."

"Cautious is good."

"I haven't done much dating since my fiancé died."

"Isn't it time you take a risk again?"

Was it? "I'll think about it."

What would Tyler think about this?

Tyler? Why was she thinking about Tyler?

If she started dating someone, she'd have to forfeit Tyler's bear hugs. She'd have to distance herself from her friend. The thought clutched her heart, pressing on it with sadness.

Gavin wrapped his arms around her, and they stared at the waterfall for a moment. "How's your book coming?"

She scrunched her lips together, thoughts of the novel already forgotten as the mystery of the missing man grew deeper. "It's not. I'm afraid I'm burned out creatively. Maybe my day has already passed."

"I don't believe that's true." His hand grazed her neck and rested there, lightly rubbing her tight muscles. "You just need to get your mind off of it for a while. Maybe you're thinking about it too hard."

Morgan slowly nodded, processing his words. "Maybe you're right. Unfortunately deadlines can't wait, though. I'm running out of time."

"We'd love to have you stay here in Perfect for as long as you'd like, especially if that would help you work on your book." He gently tilted her face to his. "Who am I kidding? *I* would love to have you stay."

Morgan was at a loss for words. She always seemed to lose her senses around Gavin and she wasn't sure if that was good or not. From the corner of her eye, she spotted the sheriff approaching and breathed a sigh of relief. Her whirlwind of emotions was the last thing she wanted to worry about.

Gavin scowled and stepped back. "How are you doing today, Sheriff?"

The sheriff shook his head and halted in front of them. "We found a body in the woods. It looks like it could be the man you described to us, Ms. Blake."

Chapter Thirteen

Morgan's heart raced. Had she heard correctly? They'd found the body?

The sheriff nodded toward the distance. "Why don't you come with me to the coroner's office? We'll need someone to identify the man."

Morgan nodded, drawing in a deep breath. With Gavin's guidance she followed the sheriff down the trail and to the street. They briskly walked to the coroner's office.

A million questions ran through her mind, as well as fear and relief. Fear that it would be bad news, and relief that maybe she would have some answers. Her anticipation grew with each step.

She crossed her arms over her chest. "Where did you find him?"

Her voice sounded strained even to her own ears. Gavin must have noticed because he squeezed her shoulder, as if to reassure her everything would be okay. The gesture only calmed her for a moment.

The sheriff tucked his shirt into his pants and sniffed. "In the woods by the river about two miles from where you said you hit him. Looks as if he may have washed up."

Could the man have been saved if they'd found him before he hit the water? Her temples pounded at the thought. "Any idea about the cause of death?"

Sheriff Lowe shook his head, his breathing heavy as he tried to briskly move his bulk. "Hopefully the coroner will be able to tell us."

They reached the next block and the sheriff's office came into view. She quickened her steps. This mystery was close to being solved. Maybe she could finally have some peace and move on.

The sheriff pushed open the heavy doors leading inside, and the frigid air conditioning assaulted them. Morgan brought her arms across her chest to ward off the cold.

"Have a seat, if you will." The sheriff pointed to two metal folding chairs. "I'll be right out with more instructions."

Morgan sank into the chair, her shoulders tense and her stomach tightening. The next hour could prove to be devastating or a relief, or maybe both. Whatever the news, at least Morgan would have some answers.

"You're looking a little pale." Gavin pulled his chair closer to her and slipped an arm behind her. "Just think, in a few hours all your questions will be answered."

Morgan drew in a deep breath and nodded. She closed her eyes, trying to sort out her thoughts and gain control of her spiraling emotions. Was it Morgan's fault the man had died? Had she really done everything she could? What kind of help had the man been asking for?

"What do you think happened to the man, Morgan?"

She pulled her eyes open and stared at the bland cinder-brick wall in front of her. The scene began replaying in her mind again. Hardly an hour went by without the haunting, movie reel-like images appearing. Each time, they seemed to urge her to remember something or serve as a call to action. "I think he was being chased."

A moment of hesitation lingered before Gavin asked his next question. "What do you think was chasing him?"

"It could have been a wild animal, a bear perhaps." She glanced up at Gavin's crystal blue eyes, remembering how he'd been such a good listener since the time they'd first met. In the short time she'd known him, he'd proven himself trustworthy. Still, she swallowed a little too hard. "Or it could have been a person."

He shifted in his seat, pulling away from her slightly. His jaw became rigid, his gaze tight. "And do you think that whatever, or whoever, was chasing the man finally caught him?"

"It's just a theory, a hunch." She let out a long sigh and ran her hands over her face. "I actually have no idea. But I just keep thinking about this man's family. I'm sure they're worried sick."

He patted her hand. "We'll get this figured out. There's nothing for you to lose sleep over."

"I hope you're right."

"Of course I am." His voice turned crisp. "Now, let's get your mind on something else. I've been meaning to tell you that your first book was my favorite. I thought the book was much better than the movie."

"You actually read my book?"

"Of course I did. All of them. Did you think Bonnie was your only fan in town?"

"I don't know if I'd say that, but I am flattered."

"I'm not flattering you. I'm telling the truth. You painted such a vivid picture of how anger can become a monster inside of us, a monster that we can lose control over." He shifted. "Where did you get the idea for that book?"

There was the standard answer she usually gave— that she got the idea for "Redemption's End" after watching a documentary on human trafficking. That was partly the truth. But her main inspiration had been her stepfather, a man who appeared perfect to the outside world. Behind closed doors, he was a different man.

Before she could answer, the sheriff appeared. Saved by Sheriff Lowe—again. Walking into the middle of uncomfortable moments seemed to be the only type of "saving" the sheriff was capable of, however.

He paused and twirled the toothpick between his teeth. "The coroner wants to do an autopsy. We have to locate the family first. He said his initial impressions are that the man died from a drug overdose, though."

"A drug overdose?" Morgan pictured the crazed look the man had in his eyes when she'd hit him. "What else did he say?"

"He also had broken rib." A man with white hair stepped from behind the sheriff and extended his hand, a warm smile on his face. "I'm Coroner Williams. Nice to meet you." He looked down at a clipboard in his hands before continuing. "It looks like Mr. Doe was approximately 24 years old. All the signs seem to say that he's been dead for about two days."

Twenty-four years old? Morgan thought. *That's only three years younger than I am.* She shook away the thought.

"But it doesn't appear he died from …" She couldn't finish her sentence.

"From being hit by a car?" The coroner's gaze flickered toward her for a moment. "No, that probably just gave him a broken rib and some bruises."

"Any idea who this man might be?" Gavin asked.

"I'm going to see what I can find out through the wire," the sheriff said. "Ms. Blake, would you mind coming to identify him as the same man you saw on the road?"

She nodded and stood.

"Would you like me to go with you?" Gavin rose from his seat.

"I'll be okay." Her answer seemed to disappoint him, but he nodded anyway.

She followed the sheriff and coroner through the hallway. They entered the examination room where a body laid on a table in the center, covered by a white sheet.

The room was cold and sterile. It smelled of chemicals she couldn't name, but that reminded her of the formaldehyde she used in high school when dissecting frogs.

Hesitantly, she walked over to the table. The coroner waited on the other side of the man, holding the sheets at the top. He waited for her permission before slowly drawing back the sheet.

Morgan sucked in a breath as a pale, swollen face came into view.

Chapter Fourteen

Morgan looked away. "It's him."

She closed her eyes, trying to erase the image of his face smeared across her windshield. But again she slipped back in time and saw his mouth forming the word "help." Whether he was drugged or not at that time, was he still coherent enough to know something wasn't right? Was he running for his life?

Coroner Williams cleared his throat, and Morgan snapped from the memories. "Is that all?"

"For now."

The sheriff led her back to the waiting room. Gavin rose when they entered, his eyes full of questions.

Morgan drew in a deep breath. "It was the same man."

Gavin pulled her into a hug. His strong arms held her up and made her feel like everything was going to be okay.

Please, Lord. Let everything be okay.

Sheriff Lowe cleared his throat and they pulled away. Morgan ran her fingers through her thick hair and turned to the sheriff.

Her eyes met his. "Is there anything I can do?"

He shook his head. "We'll get back with you if anything comes up."

Gavin directed Morgan outside and began to walk with her back to the bed and breakfast. His hand slipped around her waist, offering additional support.

"Are you going to be okay?" He pulled her closer.

She nodded. "I just hate to think …"

"Come now, Morgan. You do realize it's not your fault, don't you?"

"Something's not right." She shook her head. The man seemed to be begging for her help, even in death. "I can't put my finger on it, but there's more to the story."

She considered telling him about the dent in her car, but stopped herself. For some reason, she didn't feel right sharing that information still.

"You've been through a lot, Morgan. You just need some time to relax."

She had been through a lot. She couldn't argue there. "I suppose you're right. Maybe the stress is getting to me."

"Sure it is. Give it a few days. Things will return to normal."

Easy for him to say. He didn't unwillingly play a part in taking a man's life. Of course, according to the coroner, neither did Morgan. She still felt responsible, though.

The bed and breakfast came into view, and they strolled the rest of the way in silence. As soon as they walked onto the porch, Lindsey threw the front door open. Her forehead wrinkled with concern.

She ushered them inside. "I heard the news. Are you all right?"

"News gets around fast here." Morgan nodded. "I'm fine. A little exhausted, but fine."

Lindsey studied her face before pulling Morgan toward the dining room. "Why don't you two join me for dinner? Rick's out of town on business and I have enough food for all of us."

Enticing aromas attacked Morgan's senses as they walked past the kitchen and her stomach rebelliously rumbled. "I would hate to impose."

Lindsey waved her off. "Nonsense."

Her hunger finally won and she accepted. Morgan looked over at Gavin, hoping he would stay also.

"Your hospitality never ceases to amaze me, Lindsey." He stepped behind Morgan and laid a warm hand on her shoulder.

They sat down to homemade lasagna, a tossed salad, and garlic bread. The conversation was lighthearted and chatty as they ate, making Morgan temporarily forget about her worries. She felt so at home in this place, like she'd lived here months instead of mere days.

For dessert they migrated to the living room where Lindsey served pound cake, along with Morgan's favorite—hot chocolate. While they were talking about the places they'd always wanted to visit, the doorbell rang and Lindsey excused herself. Morgan's ears strained to hear the conversation, as she wondered if it was the sheriff bringing more news.

A familiar, masculine voice carried through the hallway. "I was hoping to find a room for the night."

"We only take guests with reservations." Lindsey's voice sounded clipped and tight.

Morgan's curiosity grew.

"I was hoping you had one room available. There doesn't appear to be any other hotels in the area."

Why did Morgan know that voice? It sounded so familiar, yet so out of place. Could it be…

"Really, we do require reservations." Lindsey's voice rose in pitch. Why did she sound so anxious?

Gavin had mentioned they weren't renting out any rooms so Morgan could have some privacy, which explained the tension.

"Don't turn away any guests on my account." Morgan stepped forward. Her eyes widened at the familiar figure donned in a black leather jacket and jeans. "Tyler?"

He grinned, a small amount of guilt evident in the lopsided sag of his lips.

Morgan closed the space between them and threw her arms around him. Just feeling his arms wrap around her waist made her feel like everything would be okay. She stepped back, just far enough to see his face. "What are you doing here?"

"Taking a couple of vacation days. You know how much I love the mountains in the fall. I … I couldn't resist."

"I can't believe you're here." Looking up into his warm eyes was enough to make all the tension she'd been feeling simply melt away. "I've been dying to talk to you."

Gavin stepped forward, his gaze bouncing back and forth between the two of them. "I take it you two know each other."

Morgan snapped back to the present. She stepped out of Tyler's embrace to address everyone around her. "Yes. This is…" She looked up at Tyler's familiar face again. "This is my best friend, Tyler Carson. Tyler, this is Gavin Antoine."

The two men shook hands.

Gavin turned to Lindsey, the action stiff and measured. "A guest of Morgan's is a guest of ours. Lindsey, could you make room for just one more person?"

Her gaze fluttered around for a moment before resting on Gavin. "Of course."

Gavin paused a moment before offering a crisp nod. "Well, we're glad to have you here in Perfect, Tyler. I know the two of you will want to catch up, so I'll be going." He turned toward Morgan. "Take care of yourself. You're looking a little pale today. I hope you're not coming down with something."

"I will."

Gavin kissed her cheek and gave Tyler a curt wave before departing.

"I'll show you to your room." Lindsey hardly made eye contact as she stepped forward. Perhaps the woman was a planner, someone who didn't do well with last minute changes in her schedule.

Morgan put a hand on her arm and waited until the woman's gaze fluttered up to hers. "Why don't you let me show him where he'll be staying, Lindsey? The room across the hall, right?"

Lindsey nodded uncertainly. Morgan glanced down and saw the woman's hand trembling. Lindsey licked her lips. "The room already has fresh sheets." Her eyes flickered to Tyler. "I think you'll be comfortable there."

Tyler's hand remained at Morgan's waist. His voice softened as he talked to Lindsey, as if he'd noticed her anxiety also. "I just appreciate you letting me stay, Lindsey. Thank you. I promise I won't be a bother."

"It's no problem." Her voice barely sounded above a whisper. "Here's a key."

Morgan took the key before grabbing Tyler's hand and leading him upstairs. She willed herself to remain quiet until they had some privacy. His presence here was an answer to prayer.

Thank you, God. You did let me catch a break.

She pushed the door open, relishing the scent of spicy aftershave as he brushed past. As soon as he stepped over the threshold, she closed the door and leaned against it. As excited as she was to see him, she had more pressing questions. "What are you doing here?"

He stood in front of her, close enough that her heart unwittingly sped. "There are some things I need to tell you, Morgan."

Her throat went dry. "About what?"

He bobbed his head toward the window, toward the darkness on the other side. "About this town."

"Perfect? It's a great town. What small towns should be. Everyone knows each other and checks on each other. Kids play together without the normal worries that people in the city have."

His eyes searched hers. "You sound like you like it here."

She shrugged. Why did she feel like she was betraying Tyler if she said yes? "It's a nice change of pace."

"Who's Gavin?"

Why did Morgan blush at his name? "He's…" What did she say? The mayor? A friend?

Tyler raised an eyebrow. "He's interested in you as more than an author."

"We've only known each other a couple of days."

"Sometimes that's all it takes." He paused. "Are you happy?"

She shrugged again. "Really, Tyler, there's nothing to be happy about. We've been talking, but I'll be leaving in a few days."

"That's what I want to talk to you about. Leaving."

The way he said the last word made her suck in a quick breath. "I don't understand."

Tyler shifted his weight, one hand going to his hip. "I don't like you being here, Morgan."

"I gathered that from the fact that you showed up here unexpectedly."

He took a step closer. "I think something's going on."

She bristled. "What do you mean?"

"What if there's a connection between all of the people in this area who've mysteriously disappeared and you being invited here?"

Morgan felt her face go pale. "What did you say?"

He repeated himself.

Morgan pinched the bridge of her nose. *People who had mysteriously disappeared.* Thoughts swirled in her head.

"What's wrong, Morgan?" Tyler placed his hands on the side of her arms to steady her.

Morgan lowered herself to the edge of his bed and poured out everything that had happened. She included her visit with Tony and her theory that John Doe was being chased.

Tyler's jaw was set in an unwavering position as she concluded. "I want you to leave."

Morgan shook her head. "It just doesn't make sense."

"There's something going on here, Morgan. From what you've told me ... there's more to that accident than meets the eye. Dents in cars don't just disappear. And most towns like this are dying, not thriving. They're getting their money from something, and it's not the coal mines anymore. If I had to guess, I'd say drugs."

"Drugs?" Morgan supposed that theory could make sense. And if John Doe had died from a drug overdose... "If there's a problem here, I should tell Gavin. He needs to know."

Tyler's eyes clouded as he bristled. "How do you know the good mayor's not involved?"

Morgan blinked. "Gavin?"

"I saw the car out front. That's his, right? The Rolls Royce. Where's he getting that kind of money?"

"Investments. He was a lawyer up in Boston for awhile." Her words sounded weak, even to her own ears.

"You believe that?"

Morgan raised her head. "Yes, I do. Why shouldn't I? Wealth doesn't always equate to crime. Some people actually earn their money and try to use it for good. Gavin's turned this town around. Even if there's some kind of drug problem going on here that still doesn't mean I'm in any danger."

"It doesn't mean you're safe, either."

She looked away. "I can't leave. Not yet."

"What do you mean you can't?"

"He asked me to help." Morgan's eyes met his. "That was the only thing the man I hit said."

"Leave it to the local authorities, Morgan. That's helping. It's their job."

"I told them. They say there's no case. They—"

"They could be in on it," Tyler finished. "Money can motivate people to do crazy things."

John Doe wasn't the only thing keeping Morgan here, she realized. "There's more, Tyler. I... I think Lindsey might be being abused by her husband."

"Why would you think that?"

"I've seen some bruises. I've seen the fear in her eyes." She shrugged. "I don't know. A gut feeling, maybe? Sometimes she just looks at me, and I feel like she's silently pleading for help. Maybe I'm here for a purpose. Maybe that purpose is to help her."

They stared at each other for a moment until weariness overtook Morgan. Her arms felt like they weighed a thousand pounds and her eyelids wouldn't stay open. Not to mention the throb that began near her forehead and spread backward.

"I have to go to bed, Tyler. I just … I don't know what to think."

His voice softened. "Get some rest."

She nodded and met his eyes. "I missed you, Tyler."

He gently rubbed her jaw line with his thumb. "I missed you too, Morgan."

***

Sometime in the middle of the night, nausea assaulted Morgan. She reached for the clock to see what time it was, but her arm went limp before she touched it. Darkness filled the room and panic swept through her.

What was wrong with her?

"Oh, Lord. Help me," she whispered, as her muscles tightened in pain again.

The nausea lingered.

Morgan threw her legs out of bed and stumbled into the bathroom. The room twirled around her, forcing her to hold on to the sink to maintain her balance. With a shaky hand, she turned on the cold water and splashed some on her face.

She lowered herself on the edge of the bathtub and waited for the spell to pass. As the pain became worse, she could hardly hold herself up.

"I need help," she whispered. She couldn't sit here all night and bear this ache.

Using every ounce of her willpower, she stood on the cold, tile floor and took baby steps to her bedroom door. Her hand clenched her stomach as sweat broke out across her forehead. Everything wobbled around her.

Tyler, she remembered. Was that just a dream or was he really staying across the hall? It was real, she decided. She could make it that far.

She took another shaky step toward the door. Her entire body longed just to curl into a ball to ease the pain, but she couldn't give in to that urge. She had to get help.

Her knees weakened with each step, but finally she reached the door. Had it always weighed so much? It took several yanks before it opened.

"Five steps," she whispered, calculating the distance she had to get to Tyler's room. "I can do that."

Each step felt like a lead weight was attached to her legs. Nausea threatened to materialize itself. Slowly. Steadily, she reminded herself.

"Three more steps."

Her breathing was haggard. She raised her leg to take another step when suddenly her knee couldn't hold the weight. She felt herself falling.

In the darkness, she hadn't realized how close she was to the stairs, but her body weight pulled her down.

Then it was black.

Chapter Fifteen

When Morgan came to again, sunlight streamed through the gauzy white curtains on two sides of her room. She lay in bed and her head pounded like a giant rammed his fist into her temples over and over.

Her vision cleared, and Coroner Williams came into view. "Am I dead?"

"Good to see you have a sense of humor." He chuckled. "Dead, no. Lucky, yes. That was a nasty fall you took. Could have been a lot worse."

Everything came rushing back to her, and she cringed. "Why are you here?"

His eyes twinkled. "Well, Ms. Blake, in small towns we don't have enough dead people for a full-time coroner. So, I'm also known as Dr. Williams."

"Pleased to meet you, Dr. Williams." She pulled herself up in bed and grasped her head as an ache pounded. Tyler appeared at her side. Just having him here made her pain more bearable. "What happened?"

"It appears you picked up a nasty bug of some sort. You had a rough night and were going in and out of consciousness. And you have a nasty cut on your forehead from your fall. Had to give you four stitches.

You're going to want to take it easy for a couple of days."

She moaned quietly as she felt the gauze on her head. "This is definitely going down as one of the worst bugs I've ever had." She sunk back into the bed. "I could sleep some more, I think."

"Probably a good idea. Luckily you have this young man here to take care of you." Dr. Williams nodded toward Tyler. "I think you'll be in good hands."

"Thank you."

Dr. Williams turned to Tyler as he packed up his stethoscope. "Keep an eye on her. Come get me at the first sign of anything strange. And make sure she rests. That will be the best medicine."

"Got it."

As soon as the doctor shut the door, Tyler sat on the edge of her bed and wiped a hair back from her forehead. "How are you?"

"I've been better."

His warm brown eyes never left hers. "You gave me quite a scare last night."

"I must be coming down with something. I've felt lousy off and on all week. It's the strangest thing because I hardly ever get sick, but I've just been feeling this all-over exhaustion lately."

"Maybe I should drive you home so you can rest."

"And leave my car here? That would not be wise, Mr. Sensible."

He cracked a smile. "I can be spontaneous sometimes, you know."

A grin touched her lips. "I know. But I like that you're sensible, so don't change too much."

He raised his eyebrows. "You like sensible men? I took you as the type who liked the flashy sort."

"You mean like Braden?"

He half-shrugged. "Yeah, like Braden."

"There are some things that even you don't know about me, Tyler." Even though she trusted him like no other, there were some things she wondered if she could ever tell him. Would he understand? Or would it ultimately hurt him?

Her eyelids began to sag.

"You should get some rest. Doctor's orders."

She nodded. "Are you staying close by?"

"Couldn't pry me away."

And with that assurance, she drifted to sleep.

***

When Morgan's breathing evened out and Tyler was sure she'd fallen asleep, he crept downstairs. Lindsey stood in the kitchen, kneading some dough while a pot full of something boiled at the stove. The scent of chicken and vegetables filled the room and caused his stomach to rumble.

Tyler paused at the breakfast bar and cleared his throat. "Thanks for your help last night."

Lindsey jumped before whirling around. Her skin looked pale and her eyes wide. Was Morgan right? Was Lindsey being abused by her husband? Tyler had been called to plenty of domestic disputes, and he knew how well some couples could cover up their problems. He couldn't stand the thought of a man purposely harming a woman, though. His dad had raised him better than that.

She patted her heart. "You scared me."

Tyler pulled up a seat at the bar. "I didn't mean to. I apologize."

She swallowed hard and nodded. "How's Morgan?"

"Sleeping again."

"Must be some bug she has. Poor thing. I don't think she's felt well since she got here." She turned back around and began working the dough. "Can I get you something to eat? To drink?"

Something about the way Lindsey said that didn't sit right with Tyler. He didn't know what. What did Lindsey know about this town? Was she aware of something illegal going on? Maybe he needed to press a little harder.

His gaze flickered toward the coffeepot. "Do you have any coffee made, by chance?"

"No, but I can make you some." She abandoned the dough and hurried toward the coffeepot. Her steps almost seemed frantic, like she couldn't get to the other side of the kitchen fast enough.

"Don't make any just for me. I'll be fine."

Her hands trembled as she began scooping out the grounds into a filter. "It's no problem. I want to make my guests comfortable. And you had a long night."

"You're a gracious hostess. Thank you."

His compliment must have hit home, because Lindsey looked up and seemed to offer the first genuine smile Tyler had seen across her face. A couple minutes later, she sat a steaming mug in front of him before returning to her cooking and baking.

He took a couple of sips and leaned back into his chair, trying to appear casual. "So, what do you think about that man Morgan hit on the way here? Crazy, isn't it?"

She didn't turn to look at him. On purpose or out of practicality? "I know. She's handled it so well. I would probably be on anti-anxiety medication by now."

"This a pretty safe town?"

"I like to think so." A deep, masculine voice cut into the room.

Tyler turned and saw a man in uniform step through the backdoor and into the kitchen. His eyes seemed to shoot laser beams at Tyler. Tyler stood and extended his hand. "I'm Tyler Carson, a friend of Morgan."

The man didn't take his hand. Instead, his fingers remained sprawled at his hips. The man obviously meant business. "I heard who you were."

"Is there a problem with me being here," he looked at the man's badge, "Sheriff Lowe?"

"We just like to keep an eye on strangers. We're a close-knit little community here. Not always trusting of outsiders, you know."

"Morgan seems to think this town's the perfect slice of American life."

"We want to keep it that way."

Tyler raised his hands. "I want to keep it that way, too. I'm just here visiting Morgan."

The sheriff stared at him another moment, his expression grim and serious—almost too much, like he was trying too hard to make his point. "Good. That's what I like to hear."

Lindsey wiped her hands on a dish towel and stepped forward. "What can I help you with, sheriff?"

The sheriff's cold gaze remained on Tyler. "Nothing. I just wanted to introduce myself to our visitor here."

With a welcoming committee like that, the town must not want to become any kind of tourist hub. Tyler nodded toward the stairway. "I'm going to take my coffee upstairs and check on Morgan. Nice meeting you, Sheriff."

He nodded. "Welcome to Perfect."

The people in this town were seeming stranger and stranger, Tyler thought as he trudged upstairs. What exactly was going on?

Tyler knew one thing. He was either going to find out or he was going to convince Morgan to leave.

***

A knock at the door awakened Morgan. She plucked an eye open in time to see Tyler cross the room and open the door. To her surprise, Gavin stood there with a tray loaded with food. "How's some chicken soup sound? It always makes me feel better when I'm sick."

She pulled herself up. "Word gets around town quickly, I take it."

"I stopped by to see if you wanted to take that walk you promised me. Lindsey caught me up to date on what had happened. I'm glad to see you're feeling better now." He sat the tray on her lap.

The soothing aroma of chicken soup filled her senses. "Looks good."

He nodded before glancing back at Tyler. "If you'd like, I'll sit with her for a few minutes and let you take a rest. Lindsey said you haven't left Morgan's side since the fall. Why don't you take a break?"

Tyler's gaze stayed on Morgan a moment before he finally nodded. "I'll go grab a bite to eat. I won't be gone long."

"Take your time," Gavin insisted.

Tyler cast another long glance at Morgan before he exited. What was that about? Did he not like Gavin? Was he really that hesitant to leave her?

"You are doing better, correct?"

She nodded. "Doctor's orders were I had to stay in bed for a couple of days, though. Making me stay in bed for that long is far worse than any sickness."

Gavin smiled. "You like staying busy, do you?"

"I've never been good about sitting around and doing nothing. It drives me crazy."

She took a spoonful of soup and raised it to her lips, blowing on it briefly before allowing herself to taste the warm liquid.

"I have an update for you on the man you hit," Gavin said.

Morgan stopped eating and sat up in bed. "And?"

"And his name is Jason Carter. He was a river guide from a town about an hour west of here. Apparently he'd set out to do some backpacking through the mountains and had been missing for about a week. The official cause of death was a drug overdose."

"What kind of drug?"

"Cocaine. They found some in his backpack, too."

Morgan shook her head, regretting the way such a young man's life had ended. "It's a shame."

"Apparently, he was a bright guy. He graduated with honors from Duke University and was taking some time out after graduation before deciding on a job. That landed him here in West Virginia."

"I guess the drugs would explain the crazed look in his eyes." She replayed the incident again in her mind. "You know, I can't tell you how relieved I feel to know it wasn't my fault."

He patted her hand. "At least now you don't have anything to worry your pretty little head over."

She took another sip of soup. "Did Jason ever stay in Perfect?"

Gavin shook his head. "Not that I know of. He set up camp in the wilderness from what I understand."

Breaking a cracker in half, she slipped it in her mouth, thinking as she chewed. "You'll have to thank Lindsey for the soup. She's been too good to me."

"She's a good woman."

"Yes, she is." Morgan studied his face for a moment. "You really do care about the people here, don't you?"

His blue eyes twinkled in pleasure. "You've met them all. I'm sure you can see how easy it is."

"Gavin, have you ever thought about moving on from Perfect to do politics on a larger scale?" Some people tried to use Morgan for her connections and, though she didn't think Gavin was doing that, she wanted to see his reaction.

"I'm quite content just to be here for now." He didn't seem eager to expound on the subject. After studying her a moment, he rose and took her tray. "You must rest. As always, it's been a pleasure seeing you."

"Thanks for stopping by," she said as he walked to the door.

Gavin Antoine was most certainly a fascinating man. But could she trust him? Was Tyler correct with his worry? There was so much to think about. So much that didn't make sense.

She argued back and forth in her mind, argued reasons to stay and to leave. Part of her wanted to believe she was in no danger, that there was a logical explanation for everything. She'd grown fond of the little town and of the people here. Now, she didn't know whom to trust.

The easy thing would be to leave. To forget about the man she hit, to forget about his plea for help, and to go home to enjoy a steady, expected life. Of course, the easy way was hardly ever the right way.

Would she really be able to live with herself knowing that she left with unanswered questions?

Despite the coroner's report the question still lingered in her mind as to whether there was more to Jason's death. If it was just a drug overdose, what did someone have to cover up? His family, at least, deserved to know.

She settled back in bed and tried to rest, tried to think.

When Tyler knocked on her door an hour later, she welcomed the relief from her thoughts.

He stepped into the room and Morgan unwittingly compared him with Gavin. Tyler was more natural in the way he acted and dressed, whereas Gavin was always prim and proper. As Tyler stepped closer to her bed, she noted the way his hair fell into his eyes and his T-shirt stretched across his broad chest. She couldn't even picture Gavin wearing a T-shirt.

He stood over her. "Feeling better?"

She swayed her head back and forth, unsure of the honest answer, before patting the space beside her bed and motioning for him to sit down. "I can't wait to get out of this room."

"Have you thought anymore about what I said?"

"I'm not going anywhere right now. That little fall ensured that."

Tyler kissed her hand and then straightened, standing from the bed. "You need to get some rest, young lady."

"Yes, sir."

"And don't fall down any stairs tonight while I'm sleeping. Understand?"

"Of course."

If only falling down stairs was her biggest worry. If only.

Chapter Sixteen

Tyler left early the next morning to drive toward the interstate. He knew the phone lines in town were supposedly down, and he needed to talk to Craig, as well as his friend at the FBI. It was going to take some hard evidence to prove to Morgan that Perfect was anything but perfect. He didn't know how many people in the town might be behind whatever scheme that was taking place, but it didn't matter. All that mattered was keeping Morgan safe.

Tyler was a good ten miles away from town before his cell phone registered any reception. He pulled to the side of the road and dialed Craig's number.

"Tyler, my man. What can I do for you? Have you discovered any dastardly deeds going on in Perfect?"

"Not yet, but I'm close. Look, I need for you to look into the death of a 24-year-old named Jason Carter." Tyler filled him in on the details.

"You think his death, supposedly a drug overdose, is really something more?"

"That's what my gut tells me. I want to know if the sheriff really reported it, as he said he did. I don't trust him yet. From what Morgan's told me, he's already bungled the investigation. I'm not sure if his inadequacies are from lack of skill or because he's hiding something."

"I'll see what I can find out."

"I'll give you a call in the morning for an update. I don't have cell reception in town."

"Really? I thought you got cell reception everywhere."

"Apparently not." Tyler paused. "I don't think Morgan's going to leave town until I have some concrete proof. She's pretty taken with the place, plus she's found a cause."

"A cause?"

"Yeah, a cause. Morgan's got a big heart—too big sometimes. When she sees someone in need, she has trouble leaving it alone. Not only does she want to help this Jason Smith guy—dead or not—but she also thinks the woman who owns the bed and breakfast where she's staying is a victim of domestic violence."

"Sounds like some serious stuff. I'll see what I can find out. I need you back here as soon as you can," Craig said. "My temporary partner talks so much I can't get a word in edgewise."

"Sorry to hear that."

"Did you tell her yet?"

Tyler's heart clenched. "No, not yet. I think I'm too late. Someone else is trying to sweep her off her feet."

"There's only one thing women like more than being swept off their feet, and that's having a rock to give them shelter from the storm. Don't do something you'll regret. Or, should I say, don't *not* do something that you'll regret."

"Convoluted, but I get it. Thanks, man."

They hung up, and Tyler thought about Craig's advice for a moment. Why wasn't he telling Morgan how he felt? It wasn't like he'd never dated before. He'd dated plenty, for that matter. It was just that Morgan... Morgan was different. She was like a once-in-a-lifetime gem. He didn't want to ruin their chances by telling her his feelings too soon or too late for that matter.

He sighed and dialed his friend, Cade, with the FBI. The two went to college together back at University of Virginia. Cade answered on the first ring.

"Tyler Carson. Just the man I wanted to talk to," Cade said. "I got your message. Tried to call you back. Went straight to voicemail."

"Yeah, apparently cell phone reception is as spotty as the deer out here." A stream running beside the road caught his attention. Tyler got out of the car and sat on a boulder overlooking the water.

"You said you needed information on Perfect, West Virginia."

Even hearing the name of the town caused Tyler's stomach to clench. "The one and only."

"I think someone took it upon themselves to name the community that because I couldn't find a thing about it. That, in and of itself, is suspicious, I'd say. Can you give me a better location?"

Tyler gave him the directions.

"I'll see what I can find out, detective."

Tyler rested his arms on his knees, his brain racing with thoughts and questions. "Can you do me another favor? Can you check out someone named Gavin Antoine?"

"I can do that for you right now. Gavin Antoine, you said?"

"That's right."

The clicking of a keyboard sounded in the background. "I've got nothing."

"Nothing?" Tyler jumped down from the rock and shuffled along the stones by the river's bank. He picked a smooth one up and skimmed it across the river. It skipped four times and then landed on the opposite bank. He repeated the motion, relieving some of the energy built up inside.

"He's not in our system. Let me check one more place." More clicking came over the line. "I can't find a record of anyone named Gavin Antoine."

Tyler's neck muscles tensed. "What do you mean?"

"I mean, not only is he not in our system, he's not in any system. I'll keep doing some digging. I know we've got a team working a drug case out there in Appalachia somewhere. All the details are hush hush at the moment."

"I understand."

"Call me in the morning. I'll see what I can find out."

"You're the best. Thanks."

Everything Morgan told him ran through his mind. What could someone be trying to cover up? The young man had died of a drug overdose, or so they said. What had really happened? And most importantly, just who was Gavin Antoine?

He cranked his engine and started back toward Perfect. He didn't want to leave Morgan alone for too long, not until he knew exactly what was going on.

.

Chapter Seventeen

When Morgan woke up later she felt refreshed and ready to get out of bed. She started her day with a long, relaxing bath and willed herself to leave the detective work to Tyler. Neither the bath nor her determination eased her worries, though.

After her bath she pulled on an olive green cable knit sweater and jeans and quietly walked across the hall. She cracked open Tyler's door and raised her eyebrows when she found no one there. Where had he gone? And why did she feel so disappointed?

With a shrug, she wandered downstairs and helped herself to the breakfast that had been laid out. Grabbing a muffin, she wandered into the living room and let her gaze peruse the bookcase as she nibbled on her pastry. She stopped by a photo album and, out of sheer curiosity, pulled it down. She sat in a nearby arm chair and rested the book on her lap.

She smiled at a picture of what had to be a young Lindsey at the beach. She squinted. Two young Lindseys? Lindsey must have a twin, Morgan mused. What fun.

She continued to flip through the album and saw more pictures of two young blondes playing on the beach or on an air boat gliding through what looked like the Everglades in Florida.

Had Lindsey grown up in Florida? Why would she lie?

Images began flashing through Morgan's mind. The bruises on Lindsey. Rick and his controlling demeanor. The trepid expression always stretched across Lindsey's features.

Had Rick forced Lindsey to lie about growing up here? Why would he do that?

"Oh!" Lindsey halted with a hand over her heart in the doorway. "I didn't realize you were in here. I didn't mean to interrupt." Her gaze hovered on the album in Morgan's hands.

"You didn't interrupt. And I hope I'm not being too nosy. I just saw this album and decided to take a peek."

Lindsey's cheeks turned rosy. "No, you're fine. I just didn't realize I'd left that album out here. I thought it was in my room. Amber must have moved it. She loves looking at old pictures."

"I can see why. These are just great. You have a twin?"

Lindsey nodded. "Yes, I do. Lori is her name."

Morgan stared down at the picture. "You can hardly tell the two of you apart."

"I have a birthmark on my neck and she doesn't. Looks wise, that's the only difference."

"Do you get to see each other a lot?"

Lindsey dropped her gaze to the floor. "Not as often as I'd like."

Morgan pointed to another picture. "And these pictures of you at the beach. You just look so happy."

A strained smile crossed her features. "The beach was a beautiful place."

"You lived there, didn't you?"

Lindsey blanched. "Why would you think that?"

"You didn't grow up here, did you, Lindsey?"

She rubbed her neck and took a step back. "I have no reason to lie about it."

Morgan rose. "Lindsey, I don't know what's going on, but if you need to talk…"

She shook her head, a little too adamantly. "There's nothing to talk about."

Morgan knew what abuse looked like. She'd seen it firsthand before. She knew the look abused women had in their eyes—the fear. And she knew the control abusive men liked to exude over their victims. Something was going on, but Morgan felt helpless to stop it.

"Lindsey—"

She shook her head again and backed out of the room. "I've got to do some laundry. Please, just put the album away and don't tell anyone you saw it."

Before Morgan could say anything else, Lindsey disappeared down the hallway.

Well, I messed up that one, didn't I?

Morgan sighed and put the album back. Maybe she shouldn't have gotten involved. But how could she just sit back and do nothing?

Maybe Gavin could do something. Maybe he could talk to Rick. Morgan would pray about possibly approaching the subject with him.

The sunlight streaming in through the windows lured her outside. Maybe a walk would help to clear her thoughts and recharge her creativity.

The day outside was perfect. Everyone else seemed to share her sentiment, Morgan noted, as an unusual amount of people wandered the streets today. Every once in a while, she noticed the citizens would stop and focus their attention on Morgan.

I'm sure it's because I'm an author, Morgan reasoned. As conceited as it sounded, it was the only explanation she could figure. Before everyone's stares unnerved her, she slipped into Bonnie's Bookstore. The redhead was chatting with another customer when Morgan entered and didn't even look up, so Morgan ducked behind a bookshelf and began browsing unnoticed.

She'd always loved books, ever since she was a girl. Just being in a bookstore revived her passion for reading a good story. She searched the titles and picked out several suspense novels that looked promising.

Bonnie's high-pitched voice caught her ear. "Oh, yes. His new book is supposed to come out next month. I can't wait."

Morgan paused, curious as to whom Bonnie was speaking.

"I've read his last book five times already. I just can't get enough of it!" the customer said.

"Really, he's such an inspiration, isn't he? A real messenger of God."

One of the books resting in Morgan's arms suddenly slipped and crashed on the floor. Both of the ladies at the counter turned to her.

"Oh, is that you, Ms. Blake?" Bonnie rushed toward her. "I didn't even hear you come in."

Morgan stepped out from behind the shelf. "It's me. I just thought I'd catch up on some of my reading." She held up the stack of books she'd collected.

"Oh, well, of course." Bonnie took the books from her hands. "Let me set them on the counter for you."

Before Morgan could object, Bonnie hurried away. The woman she spoke with slipped out, so Morgan approached the counter. Her eyes rested on a book displayed by the register and Morgan recognized it as the one Lindsey had been reading a couple of days ago. Her eyes darted to the author. Joshua A. Sutherland.

Morgan remembered hearing his name before, always associated with some philosophical movement.

Bonnie must have followed her gaze, because she picked up the book. "Read any of his stuff before?"

"No, I haven't. Is he any good?"

Bonnie's eyes widened, as if the question shocked her. "Is he good? He's phenomenal. A real life-changer. Before I read his book my life was a mess. His advice about life change is spot-on."

"And why is that?"

"He's an inspiration. He started out with nothing and then followed God's leading, and the small amount he had multiplied. He believes anyone can make something out of themselves, whether rich or poor, educated or uneducated."

Morgan stuck the book on top of her pile. "I'll get it then."

Her main reason for purchasing the book was research. She wanted to know more about what Lindsey was reading. Maybe it would give her insight into what motivated her hostess.

Bonnie tapped some buttons on the cash register. "I'm glad to see you're feeling better."

Morgan tilted her head, wry amusement building inside. "Oh? You heard I was sick?"

With a wave of her hand, Bonnie laughed it off. "It's a small town. News travels fast." She leaned in closer. "I also hear you have a friend in town."

"Yes, he's staying at the bed and breakfast." Morgan paused and twisted her lips in a grin. "But, you probably know that already, don't you?"

She had the decency to blush. "Well, yes. I had heard. Everyone around here likes to keep up with the visitors passing through town. We're so close-knit, and one can never be too careful."

"I can't argue with that." Morgan took her bag and flashed a smile at Bonnie. "Have a good day."

"Oh, you too, dear. Come back again real soon!"

Morgan shook her head, chuckling to herself as she walked on the sidewalk. Bonnie was a character, that was for sure. The town busybody.

Her mind drifted to Gavin as she walked. His office had to be located at City Hall. Before she lost all her energy, she decided to stop by for a visit. The best time to visit Gavin would be while Tyler was out.

Her footsteps quickened as the mirrored building came into view. She would only stay long enough to say hello, she decided. Her book wouldn't write itself and distractions in her life right now were plentiful.

As she stepped onto the marbled floor inside, she again drew in a breath at the extravagance around her. One day, a cute little town like this, quirks and all, would be included in one of her books. It was too … well, perfect not to be.

Morgan smiled at the pun as she approached a receptionist in the lobby.

"Hi, Ms. Blake," the young woman said. "Are you here to see the mayor?"

People in this town sure were a bit presumptuous, Morgan noted. "Yes, I am. Could you direct me to his office?"

Two flights of stairs later she was standing in front of Gavin's secretary, a pretty woman in her twenties. "Mr. Antoine is expecting you. He'll be right out, if you'd like to have a seat until he's available."

Morgan blinked. "He's expecting me?"

The secretary smiled. "The receptionist from downstairs called to say you were coming."

The laughter that escaped Morgan was that of relief. Was she paranoid or what? She'd thought for a minute Gavin had someone watching her.

Before she had the chance to sit down, Gavin appeared from a doorway on her left. His charcoal business suit gave him the aura of authority and power as he approached and planted a kiss on her cheek.

"Now, didn't the doctor tell you to stay in bed for two days?" He gave a stern look.

"Well, yes." Had she told him that? She really was losing it. "But I'm feeling much better."

"Perhaps you should have something to eat." He grasped her elbow and led her away. Looking back over his shoulder, he called to his secretary, "Order us some sandwiches. We'll take them in my private dining room."

In a whirlwind, Morgan was ushered into a cozy room with a glass top table and seated in a padded chair. Gavin took his place across the table and focused his full attention on her.

"I really must insist you go back and rest after our lunch." He leaned across the table and took her hand. "I can't have guests coming to my town and getting ill."

"Really, I'm fine." But was she? Suddenly, her head was aching...again.

Gavin seemed to sense her overwhelmed state, because he sighed and squeezed her hand. "You must forgive me. It's been a terribly busy day and I'm afraid I've carried that over into our time together. I'll try to slow down and relax a little more."

Morgan studied his face, trying to understand this man who had her so fascinated. "What keeps you so busy here, Gavin?"

He drew back slightly. "Well, a lot of things. We're in the process of renovating many of the buildings in town. Plus, we're still trying to finalize the details of the enrichment center. It's quite a large task."

"I can only imagine."

"I do hope you'll be a part of it when it opens." His eyes searched hers. "In fact, I was hoping you might become a permanent fixture around here. I know it sounds a bit forward, but when I consider you're leaving in a few days, I realize I have no time to waste."

"I'm flattered." Morgan searched for the right words, but they escaped her. His request had thrown her off guard. What was she supposed to say?

"Don't say anything for now. Just think about it."

Her headache grew worse. Hopefully that food would be here soon. As if on cue, the doors opened and two boxed lunches were delivered. They both helped themselves to the deli sandwiches from Donna's, Morgan not realizing her hunger until then.

"How's your friend doing?"

"My friend? Tyler? He's doing...fine."

"I'm sure that was a pleasant surprise, having him show up here so unexpectedly."

"He's usually not so spontaneous. He worries about me. A little too much sometimes, though he'd never admit it."

"Why would he worry about you? Is there reason to worry?"

She shook her head. "No, not really. My fiancé was his best friend, though. I think he feels like it's his duty to make sure I'm okay."

"Does he always follow you places?"

"Follow me? I wouldn't say he followed me here. He just thinks I need a bodyguard. I guess I would be an easy target for someone angry with my stepfather or even a deranged fan." She paused. "Any reason why you're asking all of these questions?"

"Forgive me. I admit that I can be a bit jealous at times. We've only known each other a short time but you've already captured my heart."

Morgan's cheeks flushed. "I'm not someone who jumps into the pool. I stick my toe in first and then slowly—painfully so—tip-toe in. Especially when it comes to relationships."

"An admirable quality to have, though I fear time isn't on our side right now." He tilted his head. "You're always welcome to extend your visit."

"The town has been very welcoming. I can't deny that."

"Do think about it." He pointed to her bag. "I can see you've been to Bonnie's. Find any good reads?"

"I did find a new author I'm really curious about. His name is Joshua Sutherland. Ever read any of his stuff before?"

"I have. Excellent writer, if I do say."

She leaned forward. "And why is that?"

"He talks about really living to our full potential, not wasting any opportunity."

"I heard he was New Age." She took another bite. As much as she struggled sometimes to think that God really loved her, she definitely believed in God and the Bible. She didn't like it when people tried to distort religion into something it wasn't.

Gavin shook his head adamantly. "Oh, no. He's very much a Christian. You'll have to tell me what you think of his book after you've read it. I think you'll find it very interesting."

"I'm more curious now than ever. I think I'll start on it when I return to the bed and breakfast. It will give me something to do while I'm confined to my bed."

Gavin looked at his watch. "Speaking of going to bed, you really should get back. Don't push yourself too hard, Morgan."

Going back to bed had never sounded so good. She rose from the table, in an agreeable mood. "You're right. I should get some rest."

He walked with her to the door. Before opening it to the outside world, he placed his hands on Morgan's shoulders. Gavin's lips suddenly came down over hers in a brief kiss. His spicy, alluring scent momentarily filled her senses and made her forget about the headache pounding at her temples. Gavin Antoine was the kind of man who could consume a woman's thoughts and, at that moment, that's exactly what he did.

He pulled away and gazed at Morgan with beaming eyes. "If it's alright, I'll stop by and visit with you tonight."

Why did she feel hesitant? Still, she said, "Okay."

"I'll see you later then." He pecked her lips once more, his gaze lingering on her. "Would you like my chauffeur to drive you back?"

Now that he mentioned it, she was getting tired. Maybe she had rushed things a bit too quickly. "That would be wonderful."

"I'll make sure he's waiting for you downstairs then."

Morgan wandered down the hallway. She needed to find a restroom. Maybe splashing her face with some cold water would revive her enough that she could stay awake until she got back to the bed and breakfast.

There were no doors marked "restroom," but an unlabeled door beside the water fountain seemed a logical guess. She pushed inside. Darkness stared back at her. A bathroom? It seemed highly unlikely based on the vast openness before her. Still, something drew her forward. Something unknown made her throat go dry. Conjured up strange, unlikely images.

Of secrets. Of death. Of evil.

She shook her head. Where had those thoughts come from? They didn't make sense.

Still, her fingers trembled as they fumbled at the wall. She couldn't leave. Something unseen seemed to pull her farther inside. The door dropped behind her, leaving her surrounded by blackness.

Her heart leapt into her throat. She scrambled backward, her hands racing over the walls. What had she been thinking? Where was that light switch? All she felt was smooth plaster, the door frame.

Finally, her fingers connected with something. She shoved the knob upward, and light filled the room.

She backed up, colliding with the wall. No, this wasn't a restroom. She wasn't sure what kind of room it was.

Several spotlights surrounded a table in the center of the room. A cabinet stood in the background. Her eyes zeroed in on the padlock over the handles. What was in that cabinet exactly? A lone chair waited in the corner.

Something on the floor beneath the table caught her eyes. Several leather straps. Belts maybe? But there was something else. Something white and familiar.

She gravitated toward the object. Her heart pounded in her ears and her breathing came in short gasps. At the table, she bent down and reached for the white hat underneath.

On the back, written in marker, were the letters JAH.

This hat belonged to the man she hit—Jason Carter. He'd been wearing it when she collided with him. How did it end up in this room in City Hall?

Chapter Eighteen

Morgan's hands shook as the growing ball of panic in her core threatened to explode into an all-out scream. She stuffed the hat into her bag from Bonnie's Books. She had to get out of here. Now.

Her legs wobbled as she hurried toward the door. She pulled at the knob and collided with someone.

A half-scream, half-gasp escaped her.

Her gaze shot up. Gavin.

She had to get a grip.

"You scared me to death!"

The distant look on his face disappeared, replaced with a look of concern. He rubbed her arms. "Forgive me. I saw you take a wrong turn and was afraid you'd gotten lost."

"I did. I was looking for a restroom, and I guessed incorrectly."

His gaze flickered behind her. Morgan held her breath, wondering if he was looking for the hat. Did Gavin know the hat was here? Did he know that Jason had been here in City Hall? Why didn't she trust him enough to ask?

"The restroom is on the other side of the hallway. Would you like me to show you?" His voice sounded as even and steady as always. Certainly he didn't know anything. Certainly.

"Please." Morgan licked her lips, all too aware of how dry her throat suddenly felt.

Gavin waited dutifully outside the restroom for her as she splashed her face with some cold water at the sink.

There was an explanation for all of this. Right? There had to be.

Things couldn't possibly be as twisted as her imagination might make them out to be. She was blowing things out of proportion. No way had they actually found Jason and brought him back here. Killed him themselves? And who exactly would have done that?

Her self-talk didn't calm her down, though.

All she could think about was talking to Tyler. And lying down. Her head suddenly felt like a giant had stomped on it.

She stepped out of the bathroom and forced a smile at Gavin. "Everything okay?"

"The room...it was just kind of odd."

"Some of the committees around town use it for their meetings. I do believe that a few of the parents let their kids have free roam of the place during the reception we had for you here a few nights ago. You know how children play."

Right. Children. They'd arranged those lights. They'd left those straps on the ground. Maybe they'd even found that hat in the woods and brought it into City Hall with them. Nothing more.

Morgan's throat felt drier than a bone. "I just need to rest."

"The elevator's waiting for you. Take care of yourself, Morgan." He ushered her through the open doors.

As Morgan rode back to Lindsey's her emotions felt like they'd been through a tornado. She had a lot of thinking to do about her heart. It was beating wildly out of control as she remembered the kiss, yet it was Tyler's picture that flashed through her mind.

She groaned and leaned back. Yes, another day in bed was just what she needed.

***

Tyler was less than pleased when he returned to the bed and breakfast and Morgan was nowhere to be found. The doctor had clearly ordered her to stay in bed, but instead she was out gallivanting around. At least, Tyler hoped that's all she was doing.

He started downstairs, ready to search for her, when he heard the front door open. A moment later, Morgan appeared in the stairway. She looked pale. Weak. He met her halfway down the stairs and helped her into her room. He didn't let go of her elbow until she'd practically collapsed on the couch. He lowered himself beside her.

"Where have you been?"

Morgan rubbed the skin between her eyes. "I've been avoiding writing my book. I…" She lowered her hand. "I found something, Tyler. I found Jason's hat."

Tyler bristled. "Where?"

"I walked into the wrong room at City Hall. It was under a table."

"I thought the town had no record of him ever passing through? Isn't that what they told you?"

"That's what they told me. But how did that hat get there? He was wearing it when I hit him."

"That's an excellent question. It makes it even more obvious that someone here isn't telling the truth. And if someone isn't telling the truth, that means they're covering up something." He shook his head, intensity seeping through him. "I talked to my friend with the FBI."

Morgan straightened. "And?"

"And there's no record of a town named Perfect in West Virginia."

"How's that possible?"

"There's something strange going on here, Morgan. Do you believe me now?"

"I believe that someone's up to no good. If I had to guess, it's Sheriff Lowe and maybe even Lindsey's husband, Rick."

Not Gavin? Tyler bit back his reply.

"I need to lay down. My head is throbbing again. I shouldn't have gone out today."

"Let me know when you wake up, okay?"

Tyler glanced at her one more time as he slipped out of her room. He loved her. He really did.

What would she do if he told her that? Would their friendship be ruined? Or would it be the best decision he ever made?

———

He was going to tell her, he decided. As soon as she was feeling better.

Chapter Nineteen

The house was quiet when Morgan awoke. She wished her heart was as peaceful as her environment. But instead she agonized over unanswered questions about everything from Jason to her impending deadline to her inability to jump into any romantic relationships. She was enough to drive *herself* crazy.

As she sat up in bed, a thought buzzed around in her head. She rubbed her temples, wondering what was so desperately trying to get her attention. She closed her eyes.

What had she been praying about before sleep claimed her? Jason Carter. Whatever was going on in this town. Gavin. Her book and her failure to complete it.

She straightened. That was it.

Somewhere in the middle of her sleep, the truth had slammed into her heart. She knew exactly why writer's block had been haunting her.

She'd stopped believing in love. In real love. The kind that was made to last, where both parties truly cared about the happiness of the other and treated each other with respect.

Each of her three published books had a romance angle to them. None of her current stories had jived because she couldn't write about something she couldn't believe in. Tears rushed to her eyes at the thought.

Why was she so afraid to reveal too much of herself, of her upbringing, of her past? There were things she'd never even told Tyler. She'd tried to share them with Braden, but he'd never truly accepted her for who she was. He'd wanted her to be the woman he'd assumed she was.

There were reasons that relationships scared her.

She needed to be honest with Tyler. Maybe the truth would be what he needed to let go of his guilt. The thought twisted her heart because she didn't want to lose their friendship. But she hadn't been fair to him.

And she had to tell him. Now.

After sliding out of bed, she freshened up before tapping on Tyler's door. The wood flew open on the second knock, and a wide-eyed Tyler stood there. His hair was disheveled and lines on his face indicated he'd been sleeping also.

Her chin quivered a moment as she realized how their relationship could change. The last thing she wanted was to lose him. He'd been her rock for the past two years.

"Can we talk?"

He squinted before running his hand through his hair, leaving even more strands standing on end. "That's funny because I wanted to talk with you also."

She resisted the urge to pat down the rebellious waves of hair, her throat dry at the thought. "It's nice outside. How about we take a walk?"

"Yeah, give me a minute. I'll meet you downstairs."

Ten minutes later Tyler joined her on the porch. Morgan's eyes roamed the town, which seemed eerily quiet at the moment. "The streets are empty."

Tyler's gaze scanned the area. "Maybe there's something going on."

"Maybe." She stole another glance at Tyler as they began walking down the quaint street. There was so much she needed to tell him. Her heart dipped, dragged down by a new heaviness. She shoved her hands into the front pockets of her jeans and let the autumn breeze ruffle her hair.

"You seem melancholy."

Morgan shrugged. "I guess I am. I've had a lot on my mind." They reached the rundown park at the end of the street, and Morgan pointed to a bench. "Want to sit for a moment?"

"Let's. There are a couple of things I was hoping we could talk about." Tyler leaned on his knees. The sun hit his face, giving it a warm glow that pulled Morgan's heartstrings. He took her hand and pulled her down beside him. He didn't let go.

Morgan swallowed, but it felt like rocks going down her throat. "Like what?"

Tyler stared at their hands, their intertwined fingers. "Morgan, I know what happened to Braden was awful. More than awful. I can understand why you said you never want to date a cop again. After losing

Braden in the line of duty like that—"

She squeezed his hand, feeling a pressing urge to correct him before he went any further. "Tyler, losing Braden in the way I did isn't the reason I'm hesitant to date a cop." Was this the opening she needed to tell him the truth?

He blinked, his rich brown eyes focused totally on her. "What do you mean?"

Could Morgan tell him the truth? She knew the answer. She could trust Tyler. He'd proven that time and time again. But would he understand…?

She released his hand and rubbed her palm on her jeans absently. "There are some things I've never told you, Tyler." Her voice cracked, and she licked her lips. Her eyes connected with his, and she silently pleaded with him to understand. "There are things I've never told anyone."

Warmth and concern saturated his gaze. "You can tell me anything, Morgan."

She bit her lip in thought for a moment. "I know. It's just…" Her life two years ago flashed into her mind, squeezing her insides. She could still remember every moment, as if it had just been yesterday. "The night that Braden was killed…"

Tyler reached for her hand again and squeezed it. "Go on."

Her heart pounded so hard that Morgan felt certain Tyler could hear it. She pulled her gaze up to meet Tyler's. "I was going to call off the wedding that night, Tyler."

He blanched before leaning toward her, his voice tinged with emotion. Surprise? Curiosity? Anger? No, not anger. He shook his head, as if trying to let the thought settle on him. "Call off the wedding? But you and Braden were so happy together. Why would you…?"

She licked her lips and let the breeze cool her face, which was warming by the second as emotions rose up, making her feel flushed. "Nothing's ever as perfect as it seems, Tyler. I don't know if you remember, but that night, I'd gone up to my parent's house."

"I do remember that."

The night played in her mind like a film reel. She still remembered her mom wearing a crisp pink blouse with a pearl necklace. Her reddish-brown hair was coiffed in its French twist. But her eyes…they were hollow. "My mom… well, we were having dinner together. My stepfather was up in D.C. for something. I looked at my mom as she sat across from me at the table, and I realized for the first time how broken she was."

"Broken?"

Lord, help me get through this.

"She'd been beat down for so long that she'd lost her will to fight."

Tyler squinted and shook his head. "I'm not following…"

"I don't have any proof that my stepdad actually hit my mom. But if he wasn't physically abusive, then he was definitely emotionally abusive and controlling. My mom, well, she was like the shrinking woman.

Whenever my stepdad came around, she looked like she wanted to curl into a ball and disappear. She put on a great front in public. She was the perfect politician's wife. Behind closed doors, it was different. I think I realized that when I was younger, but I didn't put the pieces together until I reached adulthood."

"That's terrible, Morgan. I'm really sorry. She's still with him, right?"

Morgan nodded and began tugging at a piece of peeling green paint on the bench. "I don't think she'll ever leave him."

"And that made you not want to get married to Braden?" He tilted his head, looking as if he was trying to connect the dots.

She ripped off another piece of paint and heaved in a deep breath. "There's really no easy way to say this, Tyler."

"Just say it. You can trust me."

Here goes nothing… "Tyler, Braden liked to push me around."

Tyler blanched before visibly tensing. His breathing came faster, his eyes widened. "Push you around? What do you mean? Did he hit you?" His words came out faster with each beat.

Morgan slowly nodded, willing her heart to stop racing out of control. "Yeah, he hit me. Twice. Both times were after he'd had a bad day at work. He denied going out drinking afterward, but I could smell the alcohol on him. He stopped by my place, and he was like a different person. He was just so full of rage. When certain things in his life spiraled out of control, he tried desperately to control everything else. Including me." A tear rolled down her cheek.

"I had no idea, Morgan." Tyler's voice sounded coarse, thick with emotion.

She wiped her cheeks with her sleeve. "No one did. He was apologetic afterward. He promised to never do it again. He didn't know what got into him. And I believed him. Or I wanted to believe him. Until he did it the second time." She paused. "I'm so ashamed that I stayed with him for as long as I did. I always thought abused women were weak, but then I realized just how damaged and manipulated they were instead."

Tyler grasped her hand tighter, bringing it to his lips as he lowered his head, his pain evident.

"I did mourn Braden's death. I mourned our relationship and what it could have been. As my own weaknesses and fallibility became evident, I mourned those shortcomings in myself. I vowed to never be like my mom. I found myself falling into that same pattern and letting history repeat itself. It was after that visit to my parent's house that I realized I couldn't marry Braden. I just couldn't do it. But then…"

Tyler pulled her into his arms. "Morgan, I'm so sorry. I'm so, so sorry. You could have told me. Why didn't you tell me?"

"I knew you had Braden on a pedestal. I didn't want to tarnish the image that everyone had of him. It was done. There was no changing things. So why ruin this image that people had of him? It seemed cruel. Or maybe I'm just weak."

"You're not weak, Morgan. You're… you're incredible."

Relief flooded through her. There. She'd finally said it. To someone. She'd never shared that truth about her life before. It seemed too shameful. Too destructive. "I'm sorry I didn't tell you sooner, Tyler. I kept hoping my memories of it would fade or that the whole thing would seem inconsequential. But it didn't." She glanced down at her hands, which twisted in her lap. "And I think I've been unfair to you."

"Unfair? To me? How?"

"I know you've been hanging around out of guilt. I shouldn't have let you. I should have told you earlier. I guess I feared how things would change between us if I did. But I feel like I've been holding you back."

"You haven't been holding me back, Morgan. You've never held me back. You've … made me a better person, if anything."

She couldn't look him in the eyes. She was afraid he'd see all the way to her soul. Instead, she swallowed so hard that it hurt, grabbed his hand, and squeezed. Her heart panged under the weight of her next words. "I've got to let you have your own life."

"I have my own life."

"You feel guilty because you blame yourself for Braden's death. I know you do. That's why you've appointed yourself my guardian. I've been selfish because I let you."

"Morgan—"

Tears began rolling down her cheeks, and he pulled her into his arms. She nestled her head into his chest.

Safe. That's how she felt with Tyler. His presence made her feel like she'd never get hurt. Like she could rest because someone else was watching out for her.

"So, this whole time the reason you said you didn't want to date a cop wasn't because Braden had been killed in the line of duty...?"

"I just feel like I closed myself off to a lot of relationships after he died, but especially with anyone in law enforcement. I mean, my stepdad used to be an FBI agent before he turned to politics. Then Braden."

"Not everyone in law enforcement is like that."

She pulled away for long enough to look Tyler in the eyes. "I know that. You've taught me that, Tyler. But some mindsets are hard to break." She dabbed her eyes with the edge of her sleeve. Just as she did so, a stone rolling down the mountainside caught her ear. She looked up in time to see someone walking up the road in the distance.

Rick.

Wasn't he out of town?

"Where's Rick going?" Morgan muttered.

Tyler followed her gaze. "Who's Rick?"

Morgan sat up, trying to gather her wits. Refocusing her thoughts on something other than her commitment issues had a certain appeal. "Lindsey's husband. He's supposed to be in Philadelphia on business."

Tyler's arm remained stretched over her back. Didn't she just tell him that he was free? That he could let go of his guilt? "Maybe he got back early? What's up that road?"

"The mines. They're closed down. Have been closed down for years."

"There's nothing else up that way?"

Morgan shook her head. "No, I clearly remember Gavin telling me that when I got a tour of the town."

Tyler pointed in the other direction "Maybe that woman who's been watching us out the window for the past thirty minutes could tell us."

Morgan swung her head to where Tyler pointed. "Beatrice…" Sure enough, the woman saw that Morgan had noticed her and the curtain fluttered back in place.

"You know her?"

"She's the town oddball, I suppose. She warned me to leave on the first night I got here. Said I should get out before they got me." Morgan shuddered as she remembered the woman's eerie warning. What if she wasn't crazy? In fact, what if she was the only sane person Morgan had met since coming here?

"That's unsettling."

Morgan shrugged. "Gavin said she thinks technology is taking over the town, and that modern conveniences are evil. Said she lost it when her husband died several years ago." Morgan stood. "I say we go talk to her."

Tyler stood beside her and wiped away her tears with the back of his hand. "Can we finish this conversation another time? There's something I'd really like to talk to you about. Something I've been wanting to talk to you about for awhile."

Morgan nodded. Yes, they could say their goodbyes later. Because isn't that what they were ultimately going to have to do? She felt like she was losing her best friend... because, essentially, she was. But if you loved someone, you had to set them free. That's what the old cliché said, at least.

Morgan cast a glance back toward the mine. Rick was gone. Had he seen them sitting here? Was he actually going up to the mine? Why?

Morgan and Tyler skirted the edge of town, noting that the formerly deserted streets now milled with people. They walked at a quick clip up a winding hill and eventually arrived at the shack Beatrice called home. The clapboard building teetered on the edge of town, away from any other homes. It didn't look like Beatrice had bothered to keep the place up since her husband had died. At one time it had probably been homey and welcoming.

Tyler navigated his way to the door first, before Morgan tip-toed over the porch steps, afraid she might fall through the warped, rotting wood there. The porch itself was no better. A hazard. The whole house probably should be condemned, for that matter.

Finding no doorbell, Morgan knocked loudly. A moment later, the front door flew open, and Beatrice stood on the other side. Even through the torn screen door, Morgan could see the sour expression across her face. Her wandering eye only added to the impression that something wasn't right with the woman. "Well, well. What do we have here? I haven't had any visitors in five years. What brings you two to my door?"

Morgan sucked in a deep breath. "We need some answers, Beatrice. We think you're the only who will be honest with us." Morgan implored Beatrice with her eyes. This woman could be her only chance.

Beatrice looked them both up and down before opening the door. "Come in before anyone sees you."

As soon as Morgan walked into the rickety house, the smell of must and rot assaulted her. Piles of magazines and newspapers were scattered everywhere, along with plates topped with old, moldy food. Trash littered the floor. The walls were painted a mint green color and water stains streaked from the ceiling. The electric-blue, shag carpet was dirty and matted. Her stomach dropped at the thought that anyone could live in such a mess.

"Excuse the house. Wasn't expecting company." Beatrice shuffled along in front of her and pointed to a couch. "Have a seat."

Morgan slid some magazines out of the way and carefully sat to the side of a gash in the couch cushion. Tyler sat on the other side.

Beatrice eyed them from across the room, the same sour expression wrinkling her face. "What can I get you two to drink?" Her scratchy voice sent shivers up Morgan's spine.

Morgan's stomach turned as she pictured a dirty glass. Still, she wanted to warm up to Beatrice. "Water would be fine."

"Same here," Tyler said.

When Beatrice left for the kitchen, Morgan's eyes roamed the room. Beatrice did appear to be stuck in a time warp. The magazines and newspapers around her were over ten years old. The decorations were long overdue for a change. On the wall was a picture of a much younger Beatrice posed with a handsome young man. She looked so happy in the picture, so normal.

"That's Horace and I right after we were married," Beatrice said, walking into the room. She looked at the picture and shook her head. "Sure do miss him." She clanked two glasses of ice water in front of Morgan and Tyler. "So, I take it you're not here just for a friendly visit. What can I do for you?" The softness disappeared from her voice.

Morgan stared at the glass in front of her. "You're the only one I trust to give me an honest answer."

"There's only one answer I have to give you—leave town and forget you ever came here."

Morgan studied her for a moment, taking in the seriousness in her eyes. "If you want me to leave town so badly, why are you still here?"

Beatrice's eyes clouded over. "My husband and I were two of the first people in this town. No one's going to force me to leave."

"Why should we leave, Beatrice? We need to know." Tyler leaned forward. "Please tell us."

Beatrice pursed her lips. "The people around here are crazy in the head."

Morgan's shoulders dropped at the anti-climatic answer. "People in town say the same thing about you."

She chuckled. "They say lots of stuff about me. That I don't like cars and still have an outhouse cause I don't believe in plumbing."

Morgan waited for her to continue, her heart pounding with anticipation.

"I don't have a car cause I ain't got money for a car or indoor plumbing."

"Beatrice, is Morgan in danger?" Tyler leaned on his knees, his expression tense but warm.

Morgan's throat burned as she waited for Beatrice's response. Part of her didn't want to know the answer, yet she had to.

Beatrice stared across the room, a far off look in her eyes.

"Beatrice, am I in danger?" Morgan repeated.

Beatrice shuffled to the front door and stared outside. "Seen a lot of people come and go in this town."

Morgan waited for her to continue. "Go on."

"Seen a lot of people come and then disappear into thin air, as if they were never here. Heard a lot of whispers. Seen a lot of secret meetings."

"Why are people disappearing?" Morgan stood from her seat and took a step toward Beatrice. Drugs. It had to be that drugs were being manufactured in this town somewhere by someone.

A grin curled at the side of Beatrice's mouth. "You're the writer. You figure it out. It's all right in front of you. Just don't take too long or you may not make it out."

Morgan sighed. This conversation didn't appear to be going anywhere. "Thank you for your time, Beatrice. You take care of yourself."

She pulled two twenties from her purse and left them on the table. "For your time," she explained. Tyler escorted her past Beatrice to the doorway. When she was about to open the door, Morgan paused.

"Beatrice, do you know anything about Jason Carter?"

Beatrice's face went pale at his name. "All I know is that they killed him, just like they killed my husband."

Chapter Twenty

Tyler's gut squeezed as he maneuvered down the steps from Beatrice's house. His unease could have been from his visit with a woman who could very well be loony. Or was his unrest because of the news Morgan had shared? The bombshell would be more like it.

How could he have not seen the signs of abuse?

How could Braden be such a coward?

And what did all of that mean concerning a future for him and Morgan? Were his chances ruined?

Tyler had known his friend could have a temper. But never would he have imagined his friend stooping as low as to hit a woman. Never. Anger burned inside him at the thought. He wished he could reach into the grave and give Braden a piece of his mind.

That explained a lot about Morgan. About her hesitancy to jump into another relationship. About the sad look that passed through her eyes on occasion. About why she hardly ever talked about Braden.

Morgan's estimation about why Tyler hung around couldn't be farther from the truth. He didn't hang around her out of guilt, but out of love. Couldn't she see that?

He wanted to correct her. But not now. Now he needed to convince her to leave town.

Once they were a safe distance from Beatrice's, Tyler spoke. "I don't know if she's wacko or wise."

"I'm with you."

"Morgan—" His phone beeped.

Morgan stopped and stared for a moment, her eyes lighting with realization. "Is your phone getting a signal?"

He snapped it from his belt and stared at the screen. "Just barely. Must be because we're up here a little higher than the rest of the town. It says I've got a new voicemail." He punched in his code and then put his phone to his ear. Cade's voice came through the crackly line. "Tyler...found...news...want to know...ASAP."

Morgan stared at him, waiting. He held up a finger as he dialed Cade's number. It rang once before he lost the connection. Tyler tried again and again, but the signal wasn't strong enough.

He sighed and flipped his phone shut. "My friend with the FBI found out something he thought I'd want to know."

"About Perfect?"

Or about Gavin. "Yes. I need to drive somewhere I can get a stronger signal and call him back. He said it was urgent."

"I want to go with you." Her eyes looked luminous, both fearful and determined; vulnerable and strong.

"I'm not going anywhere without you."

A weary smile flashed across her face. He reached for her hand. "Come on. Let's get to my truck." The sun was starting to sink and the air getting brisker. Tyler's gaze roamed over the town below them. What was going on? People were out and about. A lot of people, for that matter.

"Looks like Perfect has an active little social scene on weekends," Morgan muttered, her gaze following his.

They wound downward toward the town and paused on Main Street. The place had been transformed from small town to a festival, complete with booths and decorations. Pumpkins abounded, as did hay bales and scarecrows. Shop owners had put tables outside their businesses with various treats or goodies. Flags had been strung from the light poles. And people milled about with steaming Styrofoam cups in their hands.

Fall Festival. Tyler seemed to remember someone mentioning the event, but he hadn't thought much of the festivity—he'd assumed he'd be gone before then.

Several people stopped to talk to them as they made their way back to the bed and breakfast. Tyler urged Morgan to keep moving. Cade's message was urgent, setting off even more alarms in Tyler's mind. He didn't want to frighten Morgan, though. Finally, they reached the street where Tyler had parked his truck. A dunking booth had been set up on one side and a pie sale on the other. He wasn't going anywhere.

"I'd say we could take my car, but the entry way to the parking lot is swarming with kids doing a sack race and having their faces painted."

If it wouldn't sound paranoid, Tyler might think all of this was on purpose.

Morgan placed her hands on her hips and looked up at him. "What now?"

"We wait for the festival to end. Then we take a drive."

She leaned toward him, her voice low. "I have a bad feeling, Tyler."

His jaw flexed. "Yeah, me too." All of the clues seemed to be floating out there. There were just a couple of key pieces missing before Tyler could see the big picture. He shuddered to think about what image that big picture would eventually reveal.

"Holing ourselves up in the bed and breakfast probably won't do any good. Want to walk?"

No, he didn't want to take a walk. He wanted to grab Morgan and run. But when he considered his options, he realized that blending in and appearing oblivious was the best one. As long as he was with Morgan, he'd feel better.

***

Morgan took another sip of her hot chocolate and leaned against the building, watching a parade go by. The festival seemed so ideal, like the epitome of the American dream. But was there something evil simmering underneath the surface of this seemingly peaceful community? Was she really invited here simply to do a book signing and help to raise the town morale?

Tyler had urged her to be cautious. She wasn't naïve enough to believe that bad people didn't exist. Her family had been threatened because of her stepdad's political choices. A crazed fan had once tried to break into her home. In all truth, even her fiancé had used his fist to try and punish her before.

No, she wasn't naïve. There were messed up people in the world.

It wasn't the obviously crazy people that she feared. It was the wolves dressed in sheep's clothing.

Coming here for a book signing had seemed so innocent. The town itself had seemed like such a wholesome slice of America. But the warning sirens had sounded before she even arrived here, she'd just ignored them. First, Jason Carter. Then the dent disappearing from her car hood. The implication that both Lindsey and Dawn had always lived here, only to find out that they hadn't.

"What are you thinking about?" Tyler leaned close, close enough that she could feel the heat radiating from his body. Close enough that she wanted to melt into him and forget about all of her worries.

"Evil." She stole a glance at him. "I'm thinking about how things aren't always as they seem."

"No, things aren't always as they seem." His gaze caught hers, and she realized there was more to his words. Was he talking about their conversation earlier? About the guilt that kept him in Morgan's life?

"Glad to see you made it to the festival tonight."

Morgan and Tyler both jerked their heads toward the voice. Gavin stood there, looking debonair in his high-neck, cable knit sweater and crisp jeans. He seemed so out of place here. Was he out of place here?

Morgan forced herself to focus. "You guys know how to have a good time."

"That we do." His gaze remained on Morgan a second, before he turned to Tyler. "May I steal Morgan from you for a moment? I promise we won't be long, but there's something I must tell her. In private."

Morgan's throat ached. Gavin was trustworthy...wasn't he? Tyler's eyes burned into her. "That's up to Morgan."

Morgan could feel his silent "no." She appreciated that he didn't answer for her. Braden would have simply made the decision for her. No, Tyler was nothing like Braden.

"I have a few minutes," she finally said.

Tyler slowly released his grip on her hand. "I'll be here."

Gavin flashed that winsome grin. "Thank you. I promise I won't let her out of my sight."

Gavin put his hand on her back and led her down the sidewalk, through the jovial crowds, past a bluegrass band, through a group of giggling children watching a magician.

"This is some festival." Morgan attempted conversation.

"We like it."

Morgan tried to relax, but uneasiness kept her muscles tensed. Her head swam as she tried to sort out her thoughts.

Beatrice: *All I know is that they killed him, just like they killed my husband.*

Dawn: *We moved here from New Jersey.*

Amber: *I didn't like Perfect when we first moved here either.*

Jason: *Help.*

If something was going on in this town, wouldn't Gavin know about it? With everything else he had his hand in, how could he not be aware of any illegal activities—activities that were putting innocent people in this town in danger? He was a smart man, savvy to his surroundings. If something was going on, he had to be involved.

The realization caused panic to begin to snowball inside her.

She needed to get away. Find safety. The only safety she could think of right now was Tyler.

Her eyes darted around. How could she escape?

"What's wrong? You look shaken." Gavin stopped and turned Morgan to face him. Orange light from a nearby lantern tinted his skin the sickly shade of fire. Of evil.

She shook her head—probably a little too fast. "Nothing. Nothing's wrong."

He gripped her arm and glanced around before tugging her. "Come with me a moment."

Something inside screamed, *No! Kick and scream! Don't go with him!*

She looked back, scanned the crowd. Where was Tyler? Finally, she spotted him on the other side of the road, blocked by the parade. His eyes met hers, and she tried to convey her panic.

Gavin pulled her away from the festivities and onto a darkened street, one abandoned by festival-goers. Her heart raced as Gavin stepped close. His gaze shifted, as if searching a moment for listening ears, before he finally lowered his head. "I know you saw the hat today, Morgan."

Morgan swallowed hard. Her gaze skittered to the left. Where was Tyler? Blocked by the parade still, most likely. Morgan's throat burned. "I did."

"I know that you know it belonged to Jason Carter."

Her breath came in short spurts, causing her voice to crack. "You're right. Again."

"I brought the hat to City Hall. I took it from the sheriff's department, unbeknownst to Sheriff Lowe."

She backed up until her fingers scratched the brick front of the store behind her. Happy sounds from the festival drifted down the street. Yet, here in the shadows, she felt alone. Isolated. Unseen.

"Why would you do that?"

"What's going on here?" Tyler stepped around the corner, his gaze intense and hot as he stared down Gavin. As soon as Tyler appeared by her side, her heart slowed. Tyler was here. Everything would be okay.

Gavin's gaze remained unchanged. "Tyler. Perhaps you should be in on this discussion since you and Morgan are friends."

Was it Morgan's imagination or did Gavin emphasize the word "friends"?

Tyler continued scowling at Gavin. "Something's going on here, and I don't like it. Care to share anything?"

Morgan noticed how Tyler wedged himself ever-so-slightly between her and Gavin.

Gavin drew himself up. "I've put in a call to my friend with the FBI. I want him to look into the death of Jason Carter."

"Haven't your men already done that?" Tyler's voice still held an edge to it.

"They have, but I'm not confident in their results." Gavin looked to the side before stepping closer. "I have suspicions that something shady is going on."

Morgan sucked in a breath. "Why would you think that?"

"Since I arrived here in town, I've been trying to make a better way for the people here. But, when I arrived, some desperation had already set in. They were used to taking care of their own, and doing things their way."

"What are you getting at?" Tyler asked.

Gavin's jaw flexed. "I think Rick is involved with some drugs. A lot of drugs, for that matter. I think Jason Carter was in on it somehow, and that Rick paid off the sheriff to sweep everything under the rug."

Tyler shifted, the gentle giant Morgan called friend disappearing, replaced with an experienced detective. "Do you have any proof?"

Gavin shook his head. "I've been trying to gather some evidence, but I'm still an outsider here. That's why I called my friend with the FBI. It turns out the sheriff never reported Jason Carter's death after all."

Tyler's hands went to his hips. "What's the scope of this? Are Rick and the sheriff the only ones involved?"

"There may be one or two others. I'm not sure yet."

"Why did you let Morgan stay with Rick if he's involved in the drug trade?"

"I didn't know anything for sure until Tuesday evening. The call I got while she and I were having dinner was from a friend with the Bureau. And since Rick went out of town, I didn't think she'd be in any danger."

Morgan remembered seeing Rick earlier slinking toward the mines. "We saw Rick. Today. He's back in town."

Gavin's clenched his jaw. "Is he? Isn't that interesting? He told me he wouldn't be back until next week. He does seminars across the country, but I fear that's really just an excuse to distribute the drugs."

Tyler grabbed her hand and tugged her. "I don't like this. I'm getting Morgan out of here."

"Wait until the morning."

Tyler paused. "Why should we do that?"

"These roads are dangerous at night. Plus, the sheriff is taking a vacation day to go fishing. They're already suspicious of you, Tyler. Leaving too quickly will only put you on their radar."

"Mayor!" A deputy rounded the corner, his pace brisk and his voice cracking. "The sheriff told me to come get you."

Gavin bristled. "What's going on?"

The deputy stepped back and pointed in the distance. "Look. There's a fire."

Morgan lifted her head and gasped, her hand flying over her mouth. The fire consumed a home. Beatrice's…

The chatter from the festival halted as everyone stared at the flames, which ate up more and more of the building.

"Were you able to get Beatrice out?" Gavin asked.

"They're working on it now." Before the deputy could finish his sentence, an explosion rocked the streets. Tyler's arm went around her. Morgan looked up in time to see Beatrice's house completely demolished with flames.

Chapter Twenty-One

Morgan felt Tyler blanket her in his arms as the last of the flames faded. Poor Beatrice. It was no wonder her house had lit up like a matchbook. All of that junk she had was perfect kindling.

Tears escaped down Morgan's cheeks at the thought. What an awful way to die. Truly awful.

Tyler's warm breath brushed her ear. "We need to get out of here. Now."

Morgan nodded. She didn't need anyone to convince her. The nagging feeling in her gut had turned into an all-out panic. She glanced toward the bed and breakfast. The booths that had been set up there were now gone. After the fire, the festival had quickly wound down as everyone turned to stare at the flames. They'd be able to get their cars out and get on the road.

Tyler took her hand and tugged her. How long had they been standing here? Two or three hours easily. Their breath now came out in icy puffs as the temperature had dropped to an uncomfortable cold. Morgan would guess it was past midnight.

"Come on." Tyler led her back toward the bed and breakfast. Tension built across her back with each step.

Fear pricked her skin, scattering goose bumps everywhere.

As soon as they stepped inside the house, Lindsey came flying around the corner and into the kitchen. Her normal placid expression was replaced with a distraught agitation. Her eyes were red, her limbs flailing. "Have you seen Amber?"

"The last time I saw her she was getting her face painted. That was a couple of hours ago. What's going on?" Morgan laid a hand over her arm.

Lindsey pulled back, her eyes darting all over the room, her breathing fast. "She's gone. She's gone. I can't find her."

Tyler stepped forward, his hands going to his hips. "Whoa. Calm down a second. When did you last see her?"

She began pacing. "Probably two hours ago. I left her to play in the kid area while I manned the bake sale table. When I went to check on her, she was gone. I thought maybe she'd come home, but when I got here I didn't see her."

"We'll go help you look. We'll walk around town, see if she just lost track of time, okay?" Tyler's voice sounded compassionate yet authoritative. "In the meantime, why don't you tell the sheriff? Can you do that?"

Lindsey stared into space.

"Lindsey, can you find the sheriff for us?" Tyler repeated.

Finally, she nodded.

Morgan and Tyler took off, walking the streets, calling for Amber. People still milled about, but no one had seen the little girl. The unsettling feeling in Morgan's stomach continued to grow.

Lord, please let her be okay. Help us to find her.

They walked around for what seemed like two or three hours before going back to the bed and breakfast. Inside, a crowd of people had gathered. They walked in just in time to hear Sheriff Lowe say, "We'll find her, Lindsey. She can't be that far away."

Lindsey sobbed. Dawn from the café slipped an arm around her, and Lindsey buried herself in the woman's embrace.

Morgan's stomach knotted. Whoever was responsible for these abductions had involved an innocent little girl? Morgan shuddered. And where was Rick? He was in town. She'd seen him herself. He should be here now…unless he was involved somehow.

The thought squeezed the air out of her lungs.

Tyler put his hands on his hips. "Has she ever done anything like this before?"

Lindsey shook her head, her pale face making Morgan's heart heavy.

Tyler turned to the sheriff. "So, what are you calling this? A runaway?"

"A missing child. We have no reason to think it was a kidnapping. There's no sign of a forced entry. Everything appears normal and untouched."

"Would Amber have any reason to run away? Did you have a fight or did something happen that would have upset her?" Tyler spoke up.

Sheriff Lowe eyed him. Tyler tried to act casual, but Morgan could tell the detective in him was coming out. His hands were on his hips and his eyes focused on Lindsey, the way he always got when working on a case.

Lindsey shook her head. "Nothing out of the ordinary."

"Don't runaways usually leave notes?" Dawn asked.

The sheriff shrugged. "Not always."

"It doesn't make sense she would run away, but it doesn't make sense that someone would randomly kidnap her either. I mean, this is a small-town. A stranger doesn't just come here without being noticed," Morgan said.

Tyler nodded beside her. "As soon as it's daylight, maybe we should send some search parties out."

"I was just going to suggest that." Sheriff Lowe stared at Tyler for a moment as if to remind him who was in charge.

"I'll help search," Morgan stated.

Two hours later, just as the sun barely started to rise on the horizon, Sheriff Lowe gave out orders.

"You two start down that trail behind the bed and breakfast. Since you don't know the area, that's the safest option." Sheriff Lowe cast a stony glare at Tyler. "Stay on the trail. I don't want to send out another search party for you. These woods are no place to try and be a hero."

"Noted," Tyler muttered.

"Everyone needs to meet back here in three hours. I'll start gathering some more volunteers. We'll have people combing every inch of these woods before noon, Lindsey. You can count on it."

"Come on." Tyler reached for her hand. Morgan didn't hesitate to accept his firm grip as he pulled her onto the dirty path that snaked into the great unknown.

As soon as they stepped into the forest, chills raced over Morgan's skin. The farther they walked from the town, the more the forest swallowed them. The deeper the shadows loomed. The tighter her gut clinched with anxiety.

Morgan hoped Amber wasn't out here, alone and scared. No child should have to endure that kind of fear. More so, Morgan prayed she wasn't hurt. "Amber!"

Nothing except birds fluttering and leaves rustling. A deceitfully peaceful stream trickled by, seeming too carefree for the moment. Occasionally, they heard another volunteer calling for Amber, their yell echoing through the valleys of the mountainous area.

Morgan's gaze scanned the landscape around her. Moss-covered rocks dotted the rugged mountainside, along with stately trees, many consumed by twisting vines that snaked their way around every visible inch of bark. Normally, the sight wouldn't bother her. Today, it reminded Morgan of a virus that tried to consume everything in its path.

The earthy scent of moss and bark and rot filled the air. Any other time, the smells would be invigorating and fresh. Today, they seemed like the enemy, like evidence that the woods had taken someone captive.

She shook off the thought. The forest was no place to play around. It was no place for a little girl to be alone. Certainly there were bears, mountain lions and who knew what kind of other dangers?

Please, Lord, keep her safe.

Two sheriff's deputies walked parallel to them. Their paths eventually fanned out from each other, and Morgan saw no one else but Tyler.

As long as we stay on the path, we'll be okay, she reminded herself.

"What's it going to take for me to convince you to leave?" Tyler helped her over a tree blocking the path.

Leave? Now? What if God had brought her here for a reason—to help Lindsey and Amber? Despite that longing, Morgan knew she needed to get away. Just as soon as Amber was safe. "I can't leave now. Not with this."

"Morgan, you're a smart girl. Do you think this is a coincidence?"

She snapped her head toward him. "Are you suggesting that someone put Amber in danger to keep me in town?"

"You've got a big heart, Morgan. Anyone can see that. If they're going to manipulate you, this is the perfect way to do it. They're playing with your emotions."

Wasn't that the very thing that Braden had played on? Her compassion and sympathy? He knew she was forgiving—too forgiving perhaps? Would her big heart be her downfall…again?

She shook her head. She'd gotten past this. She'd learned from her mistakes and set up the proper protection to ensure that she wouldn't get hurt again. She had boundaries. And even when she'd been tempted—like with Gavin—she'd made sure to keep her distance.

"What are you thinking, Morgan?"

"I thought I had it figured out, so my heart was bulletproof."

"No one's heart is bulletproof."

"Boundaries make me feel safe."

"Some things are worth the risk." Tyler glanced at her, and Morgan's heart raced. Tyler was worth the risk, wasn't he?

All the moisture suddenly left her throat.

"When are you going to take that risk, Morgan?"

She knew he wasn't referring to the risk of leaving town, but to the risk of loving someone again. "I don't like risking my heart."

"Your heart is always safe with me."

Did he mean what she thought? Did he want more than friendship? She couldn't bring herself to ask. Instead, she whispered, "Thank you."

He gently pulled her to a halt. "I mean it, Morgan. I would never, ever do anything to hurt you. I… I love you."

Warmth spread through her heart, but only for a moment. Then the familiar fear inched in, crowded out her positive thoughts. She tried to swallow but couldn't. "I know you do, Tyler," she whispered.

He looked for a moment like he wanted to kiss her. She wanted to kiss him, also. But was she ready to trust again? Was she really ready? Instead, Tyler pressed his lips into her forehead.

Safe. Tyler had always made her feel safe.

Braden had been the risky one, always living for the next adventure. Always doing the unexpected. Always caring what others thought of him. There was nothing grounded about their relationship.

Tyler stepped back. "We've got to turn back soon. It's almost been an hour and a half."

"Poor Amber." She'd desperately wished for good news.

Tyler took his hands into hers. "Let's pray about it, Morgan." Tyler lifted up a prayer for Amber's safety. Morgan's thoughts drifted to her relationship with God again. Did she have God all wrong? Had she formed an image of God that was nothing close to the real thing? Not every man in authority was like her stepdad or Braden. Tyler was strong but gentle. Firm but loving.

She'd gotten things all wrong. God had been watching out for her. He was watching out for her now.

My grace is sufficient for you, for my power is made perfect in weakness. Therefore I will boast all the more gladly about my weaknesses, so that Christ's power may rest on me.

There was that verse again. In our weakest moments, God shined the brightest, didn't He?

When Tyler said amen, she opened her eyes and wiped away the tears that streamed down her cheeks.

Tyler tilted his head in confusion and didn't let go of her hands.

"God loves me in the middle of my weakness, doesn't he?"

"He died because of our weaknesses, Morgan."

She drew in a deep breath. *I'm sorry, Lord, that I had you all wrong.*

Tyler peered at her. "You ready to start back?"

Morgan nodded.

"Just one more glance around." She climbed onto a boulder and let her gaze wander the area. She didn't want to give up on finding Amber. She wanted to hold on to hope that the girl was okay.

Something in the distance caught her eye. A flash of color—bright red. The color was out of place here in the forest. It was quite a bit off the trail, out of sight from anyone who might be hiking this path. "What's that? Over there beyond that cluster of trees?"

Tyler climbed up beside her. "Could be litter."

"Could be Amber." Morgan knew she'd promised to stay on the trail, but she couldn't. She dodged roots and trees and rocks. Tyler stayed steady at her side. Her breaths came out in spurts as she pushed herself through the wilderness.

The red remained tight on her radar. Tyler was right—it could merely be some trash left over by some hikers. Or it could be a clue as to where Amber had gone.

The ground leveled for a moment, and they reached a natural wall of rock. "Can you help me over this?"

Tyler boosted her to the top before easily scaling the formation himself. Morgan stood, ready to find some answers. Instead, she sucked in a breath. The sound teetered on a scream.

The red wasn't Amber. It wasn't trash.

No, the red belonged to a graveyard of skeletons and decomposing bodies.

On top of the tangled mass laid Jason Carter.

Chapter Twenty-Two

Morgan buried her face in Tyler's chest, trying to erase the horrible images before her. She'd never forget the look and smell of the dumpsite. There had to be twenty bodies there, some mere skeletons, others only in the process of decaying. The smell of death drifted upward. She hadn't recognized it earlier, but now that the wind shifted directions, there was no denying the scent.

Her theory that something evil simmered below the surface of the town had been a gross underestimation. Evil didn't simmer in Perfect—it consumed this place. Evil like Morgan had never seen.

"What's going on here, Tyler?" She clung to him, afraid she might pass out if she didn't.

"In my years as a detective, I've never seen anything like this. Now do you believe me when I say you've got to get out of here?"

Morgan nodded, numbness replacing her fear. But only for a moment. When her fear returned, the emotion felt stronger than ever. Terror like she'd never felt before. Terror that consumed her.

These people had been killed. Their deaths had been covered up. Their bodies had been dumped. And someone in Perfect—or a couple of someones—were behind the atrocity.

Tyler grasped the sides of her arms and leaned down until they were eye to eye. "Listen to me. We're going to go back up there and act like nothing's wrong. Then you're going to get your things and leave, no questions asked. Say you have a media appearance you'd forgotten about. Anything. You've just got to go."

Her heart lurched as she stared into Tyler's eyes. This man loved her. She'd been denying it for a long time, but she loved him, too. The thought of something happening to him made tears pop to her eyes. She couldn't lose someone else she loved. "And you?"

"I'm going to get help. I can't handle this alone. And it's out of my jurisdiction. I'll call my friend with the FBI again. I'll let them handle it." He leaned in closer, using his thumb to wipe away her tears. "Do you understand?"

Morgan nodded, feeling frozen with fear.

"Now, we've got to get back up there before someone suspects something. Okay?"

"I'm scared, Tyler." Her voice trembled as the reality of the situation sank in. Something bad was going on here in Perfect. Something horrifically bad.

"I'm not going to let anything happen to you, Morgan."

She shook her head, trying to erase the grief that rushed back to her. The memories of losing Braden, even with his issues, felt like a punch in the gut. He'd been killed in the line of duty. It could easily happen to

Tyler also. "Don't let anything happen to yourself either. Promise me?"

"I promise you." He pulled her into a tight hug — but only for a moment. "Come on. We've got to walk fast. When we get back to the bed and breakfast, grab only what you need and get to your car. I'll distract the sheriff while you do it. As soon as I know you're gone, I'll follow behind you."

"I can't leave without you."

"You can. You have to. I'm a big boy. I can take care of myself."

Morgan's mind raced as they hurried up the trail. Act normal, she reminded herself. Act like you didn't see anything.

But how could she act like she hadn't seen that massive grave? Who could be behind this? Rick? Sheriff Lowe? Would they really stoop this low?

The end of the trail appeared ahead. Sunlight filtered through the clearing, and Morgan could see crowds of people gathered. The sheriff spoke to them through a bullhorn, giving directives to new search parties.

Tyler leaned close, his breath hot on her ear. "Remember — normal. Be polite, but then get your things and get on the road. Don't even say goodbye."

Morgan nodded, trying to gather her wits and her strength.

"Promise me that you'll leave after me."

"I promise."

When they emerged, Lindsey turned toward them, tears flowing down her cheeks.

"I'm so sorry, Lindsey." Morgan shook her head. Lindsey collapsed to the ground in tears, and Morgan knelt beside her and pulled the woman into a hug.

"Where could she be?" The woman's voice cracked with emotion and grief. Morgan couldn't even begin to understand her pain.

"I don't know. But the sheriff will find her. I know he will."

Lindsey pulled away, a new emotion in her eyes. "You're right, Morgan," she whispered. "He's no good."

Morgan's heart lurched. What did Lindsey mean? How could she leave now after Lindsey admitted that to her?

It didn't matter. She had to. She'd promised Tyler. She knew that whatever was going on in this town, Morgan and Tyler couldn't face it alone, and, right now, Morgan wasn't sure who to trust. They needed to call in the authorities.

"He looks like he's doing a great job right now."

"Oh, Morgan, what am I going to do?" She sobbed again.

"You're going to get through this. We're going to hope for the best."

Lindsey nodded, and Morgan helped her back to her feet. Morgan glanced around as they stood and noticed the stares from the crowd. Any of these people could be behind the mass grave out in the woods. Chills shot through her again, and her heart sped. All of her intuition screamed, "Danger!"

"I need to go inside a moment. Concentrate on finding Amber, okay? Keep your thoughts positive."

Lindsey nodded.

Morgan gave a final glance at Tyler before slipping inside. She hurried past the crowd gathered there, went upstairs and grabbed her laptop and purse. She didn't care about anything else. The less she had in her hands, the faster she could get away without rousing suspicions. The question now was how could she get back downstairs and to her car without anyone noticing her?

She glanced out the window at the sheriff as he continued to instruct the crowd. The group from inside poured out the backdoor, gravitating toward the sheriff. This was her chance.

She drew in a deep breath before hurrying downstairs and out the front door. Her hands trembled, causing her keys to jangle together.

Get a grip, Morgan.

As she stepped off the porch, she glanced back at the crowd again. No one seemed to notice her.

She let out the breath she held. Only a few more steps and she'd be at her car. She'd get out of town, hop on the interstate and find some help.

She turned back and collided with someone.

She gasped in surprise, her hand flying over her heart.

She raised her eyes, already knowing who she'd run into. Sheriff Lowe.

"Going somewhere?" He pointed to her laptop.

Casual, Morgan. Casual.

Morgan shrugged. "I just remembered that I need to call my literary agent. I've got an appearance on a morning talk show tomorrow. I nearly forgot about it."

"You were going to leave without as much as a goodbye to everyone?"

She swallowed, her saliva burning her throat. "My suitcase is still here. I just needed to slip away for a day. With everything going on here, I didn't want to take the attention away from Amber. Finding her is most important."

"So you'll be returning?"

Morgan forced a smile. "Of course. It's just that I don't want to make NBC mad at me, and standing them up for an interview would do just that."

He stepped back and nodded. "Understandable."

Her heart slowed a moment. He believed her. She was going to escape. Part of her had feared he wouldn't let her go. Silly, she chided herself. Paranoia was kicking in.

She climbed into her car, placing her computer in the passenger seat. As she closed the door, she waved at the sheriff, praying she looked convincing. He raised his hand in a wave.

Morgan slipped her keys into the ignition and twisted. Nothing.

What? No, no, no…

She tried again.

Nothing.

She threw her head back into the seat. Someone had tampered with her car. She wasn't going anywhere.

Chapter Twenty-Three

Sheriff Lowe leaned against her door, peering down at her. "Is there a problem?"

"My car won't start." Did the sheriff already know that? If Morgan had to guess, she'd say, "yes."

He extended his pudgy hand. "Would you like me to try?"

"Sure. Maybe you've got the magic touch." She slipped out.

"I have been told that before." He slid inside and tried the ignition. Nothing happened. "Perhaps your battery is dead?"

"Is Tony's open?"

The sheriff shook his head. "Tony's in one of the search parties that are out. You'll have to wait until he returns."

"What's going on?" Tyler stepped forward, his hands on his hips.

"My car isn't working. Battery maybe?"

"Really?" His voice held a crispness that only Morgan would recognize. He wasn't buying it, either. "How about if I drive you?"

"I would love that."

He nodded toward the street. "My car's just over …" He paused. Blinked. Bristled. "It was right there on the street just this morning."

Sheriff Lowe nodded toward the road. "That your vehicle that was parked there?"

"You mean, the one with Virginia plates?" Sarcasm tinged his voice. "Yeah, that was mine."

"It was in a tow zone."

"A tow zone? I didn't see any signs indicating that." Tyler stomped across the grass, the sheriff following behind him.

Sheriff Lowe pointed to a shiny metal pole. "There's the sign. Plain as day."

Morgan's gaze traveled to the fresh dirt at the sign's base. "Did you just put the sign there?"

The sheriff's eyes glimmered, and his lips curled in something close to a smirk. "Now that wouldn't be very nice, would it?"

Tyler's jaw clenched, and Morgan could tell it was taking everything in him not to throttle the sheriff. "Since I didn't realize I'd parked in a 'no-parking zone,' how can I get my car back?"

The sheriff hiked his pants up toward his overflowing stomach and sniffed. "The impound lot is closed until Monday."

Tyler's hand knotted in a fist. "Closed? You've got to be kidding me."

The sheriff shrugged. "This isn't a big city. We do things at a slower pace around here than you city folks are used to."

Morgan stepped forward and kept her voice even. "Can't you make an exception just this once?"

"The law is the law. Besides, you two wanting to get out of town so fast makes me wonder if you had something to do with the disappearance of little Amber."

Morgan sucked in a breath, feeling like she'd been punched in the gut. "You've got to be kidding me. You can't possibly think that."

"You two are the only strangers in town. Makes the most sense. Didn't have any trouble until Mr. Carson trotted into town. Seems suspicious to me."

Morgan scanned the crowds. "Where's Gavin? I want to speak with him."

"I'm glad you brought Gavin up because I have two men over at his place right now investigating." The afternoon sun hit the sheriff's face at an angle that masked his eyes and elongated his features. Just for a moment, Morgan thought of a cartoon image of the devil. She shook the thought out of her mind.

"Investigating?"

The sheriff nodded. "He's disappeared also. There are signs of a struggle in his house. Even some blood."

Morgan squeezed her eyes shut. Had they gotten to Gavin also? Would they get Morgan and Tyler next? And who exactly were "they"? Rick? The sheriff? Who else? "No…"

"We're still trying to figure out which side of the law he's on. Two people disappearing in the same day seems suspicious."

"I'd say," Tyler muttered.

"Speaking of which, you two need to stick around until we have some answers. Got it? You're both persons of interest." The sheriff sneered at Tyler. "Especially you, Mr. Carson."

Tyler stared at him, the lines on his face hard and unyielding. Morgan could tell he was using every ounce of his self-control right now.

"Do you understand?" the sheriff repeated.

Tyler offered a curt nod. "Of course."

Tyler and Morgan exchanged a glance. They weren't going to be getting out of Perfect today. Maybe not ever.

Chapter Twenty-Four

Morgan huddled in the corner of the couch in her suite, letting reality wash over her again and again.

Gavin. After last night, she believed he was innocent in all of this. How he could be… dead? Even the thought of it made shivers wrack her body. If they killed Gavin, certainly they wouldn't hesitate to kill Morgan and Tyler also.

Without their vehicles, they were trapped in this town, surrounded by miles and miles of nothing but woods and mountains. Their cell phones didn't work, and they had no idea who their allies were.

Despair threatened to bite deep. To grab a hold of her soul and not let go.

Tyler paced the room. "When I came around the side of the house to find you, I noticed something. The phone lines were never down in this town, Morgan."

Morgan pulled her knees to her chest, fighting the panic that was growing from within. "What do you mean? I tried them. The phone didn't work."

"It's because the phone lines have been cut." He stopped and waited for her reaction.

"How…?"

"I saw the line outside the house. Clearly cut. Someone didn't want you making phone calls outside of this town."

Shivers began jerking her muscles as her heart sped. She raked a hand through her hair. "I don't know what's going on, but I don't like it."

Tyler paused from pacing the room. "We need a plan."

"I thought that's what you were doing—figuring one out." Morgan knew he needed quiet to process his thoughts, so she'd tried to give it to him.

"The problem is that every plan I come up with has too many unknowns. Too many ways for you to get hurt."

"I'm tougher than you think I am, Tyler."

He glanced her way and shook his head. "I never said you weren't tough."

"You're acting like it now."

"I don't want you to get hurt." His voice contained a mix of worry and agitation. Morgan knew Tyler well enough to realize that he wasn't agitated with her, though. He just wanted to protect her and the pressure he put on himself to do so had pulled his nerves thin.

"I got us into this mess, and I'm not going to stay here like a sitting duck. I'll do whatever I have to do."

Tense silence stretched between them. Morgan sighed and pushed herself into the couch. What could they do? She definitely had no plan—no good one, at least. Finally, she took a sip of her hot chocolate, the only thing that seemed to warm her from both the chill in the air and the chill that stared at her gut level and emanated outward. Her eyes felt droopy suddenly.

"Something about drinking a warm drink must make me tired."

Tyler stopped pacing for long enough to stare at her. "What did you just say?"

"That drinking warm drinks must make me tired. Why?"

He took the mug from her hands, sloshing the drink into the bathroom sink. "Don't drink any more of that hot chocolate, Morgan."

She pulled her gaze from the mug and slowly met Tyler's. "You don't think…"

He nodded. "I think someone's putting something in your drinks. Think about it. You feel bad every time you eat something they've prepared for you."

She squeezed her eyes closed. Could this get any worse? She didn't want to know. "Is Lindsey in on this, too?"

"At this point, we don't know who to trust."

She paced across the room, hating feeling helpless. What were they going to do? How would they get out of town without a car? Had someone killed Gavin? Was that the fate planned for Morgan and Tyler also? Her heart thudded when she thought about something happening to Tyler. It would be her fault. She was the reason he'd come to Perfect. His gut had told him something was wrong, and she'd dismissed him.

She pinched the skin between her eyes. "I'm sorry, Tyler," she muttered.

At once, Tyler's arms wrapped around her and, just for a second, she felt safe. His steady heartbeat pounded in her ear. His woodsy scent, so familiar, calmed her frenzy of nerves. "It's not your fault. You didn't do any of this."

"I should have listened to you. I should have known."

"How? How would you have known any of this?"

"You did."

He shook his head. "No, I didn't know. I just feared something was off. I had no idea the scope of it."

She stepped back, her throat dry. "Tyler, you always make me feel...safe. Protected. Thank you."

His gaze caught hers. "I want you to always feel safe with me. I wish I could have protected you from ... from Braden." He looked away for a moment, his lips twisting in regret. "I had no idea, Morgan, and I'm so sorry for that."

"You didn't know. No one did. And I was in denial." She stepped back and wrapped her arms over her chest. "I think that's why I'm having such a hard time with this book I'm writing, Tyler. All of my books have some type of romantic element that helps to drive the plot. But, after Braden, I stopped believing in love."

But you're making me believe in love all over again.

Wait. Where did that realization come from? Was it true?

Looking at him, she knew it was. Every time she saw Tyler, her heart filled with love.

And the thought of something happening to him, of never having the chance to explore what might develop between them, twisted her heart. She knew that loving again felt risky but, wasn't love worth the risk? She couldn't hide behind the past forever.

Tyler stepped closer, his eyes warm and full of…love? "There are good men out there, Morgan. Men who'd never hurt you. Who'd cherish you."

Something in Tyler's gaze pulled Morgan to him. She had the crazy urge to confess her love to him, then and there. Gavin… well, Gavin had reminded her of Braden. He'd reminded her of the thrill of romance. Tyler reminded her of love's steadfastness and strength, though.

"Tyler…"

Their lips connected—Morgan wasn't sure who initiated it. She only knew that electricity charged through her, tingling her nerves all the way to her toes. She could easily see herself kissing Tyler for a long time…for the rest of her life. Why hadn't she realized her feelings before?

A knock at the door broke the moment. They jumped back, breathless. Morgan ran a finger over her lips as her cheeks flushed. They shared a quick smile before Tyler nudged her behind him. He walked to the door and cracked it open just a sliver.

"Lindsey. Is there an update?" He opened the door wider.

A stone-faced Lindsey stood there, looking like an empty shell of a woman. What had Rick done to this woman? And how could Morgan possibly help?

Lindsey licked her dry, cracking lips. "No update. No one seems to know anything."

Morgan stepped closer. "Is there anything else we can do for you?"

"Just pray."

Morgan nodded. "We've been praying. We'll continue to do so."

"The sheriff found Gavin."

Morgan's muscles sagged for a moment. "I'm so glad. What happened?"

Her face remained lifeless. "He's dead."

Morgan gasped, her hand flying over her mouth. "Dead?"

"They found him in the woods. From what I hear, he was shot multiple times."

"Lindsey…"

"Let me know if you need anything." She turned lethargically and started down the stairs.

Tyler shut the door, the tension in the room tighter than ever. Morgan and Tyler locked gazes. Words weren't needed to express how dire the situation had grown.

Gavin. Dead? He'd been trying to turn this place around, trying to help the people and give them hope. Why would someone have killed him?

Morgan paced the room. The book she'd purchased yesterday suddenly slipped off the table. She picked it up and absently flapped open the cover as she placed it on the dresser. Her gaze skidded to a halt as she skimmed the author biography on the back flap. There was no picture, but…

She sucked in a quick breath.

Tyler closed in behind her. "What is it?"

She shook her head and pointed to the copy. "It can't be…"

"What, Morgan? What?"

She swiveled, and her eyes fluttered up to Tyler's. "Joshua Sutherland. It says he ran for senate in the state of Virginia. I thought the name sounded familiar, and I vaguely remember someone running with an independent political party against my stepfather when he was first elected. He... he was a motivational speaker. He had a small following, but he didn't get much attention. No one considered him a major player. Tall, slim, with dark hair. He'd probably be in his early forties now."

"Okay..."

"It says here that he does Seminars for Life. Tyler, Rick does Seminars for Life. What if Rick ran against my stepfather for senate? What if it wasn't a coincidence that they invited me here, but they want some kind of revenge?"

"I agree." He took the book from her and studied the biography himself. "This is getting stranger and more twisted by the second. One way or another, we're getting out of here tonight."

"How? We don't have a vehicle."

"I'll hotwire a car if I have to. Hiking through the wilderness would even be safer. I just know we've got to go. As soon as everyone goes home for the night, we're going to make a getaway."

"I have a bad feeling, Tyler."

"Do you trust me?"

She nodded.

"Then don't worry. Let me do the worrying. I'm going to take care of you."

"Don't leave."

He pulled her into a bear hug. "I won't. I'll stay on the couch, okay?"

Morgan nodded, trying to will away the terror that shook her limbs. Tyler stepped back. "Get some rest. You're going to need your strength, okay?"

***

Morgan tried to sleep but couldn't. She was all too aware of every noise, every creak, every murmured conversation outside. By nightfall, no one had found Amber still. Heavy clouds had invaded the sky along with the evening darkness, effectively wrapping up the search parties. Finally, shortly after midnight, everyone left and an electrifying thunderstorm claimed the air.

Morgan watched the digital clock beside her bed, each minute inching them closer to an escape. Finally, at two a.m., she threw the covers off. She hadn't rested a wink. How could she when lives hung in the balance?

"You ready for this?" Tyler shoved his gun into the holster beneath his black leather jacket. His face looked grey in the dim light of the room, but even then Morgan could see the tight lines of worry around his eyes and on his forehead.

Morgan nodded, trying to ward away the panic that threatened to seize her. She'd donned all black clothing—layers of it—and tennis shoes. She'd leave all of her things here. They didn't matter. No, there were more important things at stake.

She and Tyler couldn't mess up tonight. They had one chance to get this right. Failure could mean… Morgan shuddered… failure could mean death.

"Let's pray first." Tyler slipped his hand around her neck and pulled her forward until her forehead touched his. "Lord, you're the only one who can get us out of this. Be with us. Guide our steps. Blind the eyes of those who want to do us harm."

They whispered "amen." Slowly, they opened the door and began to descend downstairs. Just as Tyler's foot came down on the last step, Morgan remembered the creak. Too late. The wood groaned under his weight.

They both froze, waiting to see if anyone had heard them. Nothing.

Tyler took her hand and pulled her toward the back door. Lightning flashed outside and thunder clapped, vibrating the house's pictures and breakables. Just a few more steps. A few more steps, and they'd be at the back door. They could make a run for it.

They crept into the kitchen, where boxes of tissues and leftover food from the search parties made it appear that bombs had exploded throughout the room.

Just a few more steps.

Just as Tyler's hand reached the door, Lindsey stepped out of the shadows. Her eyes looked red and dazed. Her mouth remained in a straight line and her voice fell flat.

"No one ever gets out alive," she mumbled.

Morgan backed up, toward Tyler. "What are you talking about?"

"No one leaves Perfect. They die trying."

"Lindsey, you're not making sense." Even as Morgan said the words, the truth began to twirl in her head with an almost dizzying effect.

"First, he gained our trust. Then he gave us jobs until he controlled our finances. He got us involved in illegal activity, and if we don't listen to him, he'll take away everything we love."

Chills scattered over Morgan.

"Now he's got Amber."

Rick. He'd taken his own daughter—probably as a way of punishing Lindsey. "Then we need to call in the authorities. Get some help in here."

"It wouldn't do any good."

Morgan's stomach clinched. "Oh, Lindsey. Let us help you."

"I was just a kid myself. My parents had died in a car accident, and I was in a major depression when I discovered Seminars for Life and Joshua Sutherland. I felt hope for the first time in months. He promised me the world, and I thought he'd given it to me. I got pregnant with his baby when I was only fifteen. He let me stay in Florida for awhile—he even sent me money, but then he told me that a new life awaited me here in Perfect. So Amber and I moved here. We were so happy at first. But then things began going downhill. Especially when I found out about his other wives."

Morgan sucked in a breath. "Other wives?"

"He has several wives. When he tires of one, he passes that wife off to one of his lackey disciples and moves on to someone new."

"Come with us."

"Not without Amber." She looked out the window just as lightning cracked the sky again. "You only have one chance of getting out of here. Joshua will have his men watching you. You wondered why we have so many sheriff's deputies here? It's because they're all Joshua's eyes and ears."

Tension continued to grip Morgan's every muscle, her every nerve. Don't let it claim your thoughts, Morgan. Stay strong. Tyler squeezed her hand, as if he knew the war that raged inside her.

"Stay in the tree line," Lindsey whispered. "Wait until you get cell phone reception—if they don't find you before that. Then call for help." She pressed a key into Morgan's hand. "My job is to transport things into the mines. Here's a key. Stay to the right once you get inside and you'll eventually veer off into a cave that will take you to the other side of the mountain. If you get that far, you should be safe."

"Why are you helping us, Lindsey?" Tyler asked.

"Because when you escape here, I want you to find my twin sister and tell her that I'm sorry, and that I love her." She swallowed and handed Morgan a paper with an address scribbled across it. "Now go. They'll be watching for you."

Chapter Twenty-Five

Lightning flashed outside and thunder clapped. Morgan shivered, trying to keep her breathing steady, to stay calm. Tyler's touch helped. His grasp on her hand tightened.

"You ready?"

"Ready as I'll ever be."

He tugged her forward and pulled open the backdoor. Sheets of rain washed down. The rain would be their friend and enemy, helping to conceal them but making their journey treacherous. "Let's go!"

At once, they sprinted from the porch and toward the tree line. The lightning waited to flash again until they were in the forest. Thank God.

Morgan twisted her neck for one glance back. Lightning ripped through the sky for just long enough to illuminate a crowd of people gathered on the streets.

Morgan's stomach dropped. Perfect was… a cult. How could she not have seen it before? This wasn't about one or two evil men. It was about one or two evil men who'd brainwashed an entire community.

Fear squeezed her. Thankfully, Tyler had her hand. He led her around oaks and boulders and roots and underbrush. Mud coated her jeans, made her slip. But Tyler was always there to pull her up.

She loved him. She had no doubt that she loved this man. She only prayed she'd have the chance to tell him.

Through the pounding rain, a gunshot rang out. Tyler pulled her behind the shelter of a large oak tree. Rain slicked her hair to her face, made her clothes cling to her already icy skin. A cool breeze cut all the way to the bone, caused her teeth to chatter.

She ignored those things. She could deal with discomfort if that's what it took to stay alive.

Tyler squeezed in close. Morgan's heart beat double-time at his nearness.

"Do you think we can trust Lindsey?" he whispered.

"Do we have any choice at this point?" Just as the words left her mouth, a mix of mud and rock slid down the mountain in a wash of rain water and debris. The reality that they could, at any moment, encounter a cliff or steep drop off in this darkness hit Morgan. These mountains were a force to be reckoned with, an enemy all their own.

"You're right. We've got to get out of this rain. We'll stay as close to the tree line as we can and make our way up to the mine. We're going to have to lift up some major prayers on this one."

"I've been praying. Believe me." She turned around to face him, and her throat went dry as she looked up into his eyes. His lips came down over hers, and warmth spread through her. Her head spun from the burst of electricity between them. As quickly as the kiss started, it ended.

"I love you, Morgan Blake."

"I love you, too, Tyler Carson. No matter what happens, remember that."

"Nothing's going to happen. Understand? There are going to be more of those kisses to look forward to." He pecked her lips again. "Are you ready? I don't know how much time we have."

She nodded, her lips still tingling. Hope surged in her heart. Love. Love was worth fighting for. So was life.

Lightning flashed again, and Morgan saw a sheriff's cruiser in the distance. Had Lindsey reported them? Was this a trap? Or had the sheriff and his men really just been watching their every move? Morgan prayed it was the later.

Tyler halted in front of her, and Morgan collided into his back. "What—?"

She stopped mid-question. Widow Falls thundered below them. In the murkiness of the thunderstorm, they could have walked right off the cliff and fallen to their deaths. Just looking down to the swirling water below made Morgan's head spin.

"What do we do?"

"It would take too long and be too dangerous to go around. There are too many walls to scale. It's too slick. We're going to have to creep closer to the road to get around this. There's no other choice."

Fear gripped her. She could do this. She could. "Okay."

Staying low, they crept toward the road. Each step felt precarious. One misstep could lead to their death. Morgan wasn't ready to die yet.

Tyler jerked her behind a rock just as headlights brushed the area. As soon as the car rolled past, they began creeping along the strip of woods again. A cliff dropped off on one side; the street on the other.

Finally, the mine entrance appeared ahead. They were almost there.

Dogs barked in the background. Did they have hounds out looking for them, following their scent?

They hunkered down at the edge of the road. Nothing. No one. No one visible, at least.

On the count of three, they sprinted across the asphalt. Rain pelted them. Thunder shook the ground. The noises disguised the sound of anyone on their trail.

They sprinted until they reached the entrance of the mine. For a moment, the rock above gave them shelter from the downpour. Tyler's hands were surprisingly steady as he jammed the key into the lock and pulled the gate open. They slipped inside, the gate clicking shut behind them.

They were safe. For a moment, at least.

A cool, earthy dampness floated up from the depths of the mountain.

Along with blackness. Inky, blinding darkness that seemed to reach out and grab them.

A light sliced through the air, illuminating the cavernous space around them. A flashlight. Tyler had remembered a flashlight. Morgan's racing heart calmed for a moment.

The flashlight's beam spotlighted a door in the distance. Tyler tugged her across the slick stone floor. Morgan craned her head, searching for signs that anyone had followed them. So far, so good.

Tyler unlocked this door with the same key Lindsey had given them. The same damp odor drifted out, along with a new smell, one that reminded Morgan of a closet full of cleaning solution.

Morgan scrambled into the new space, Tyler right on her heels. He slammed the door shut and jammed the lock in place. The flashlight showed a switch on the wall. Tyler flipped it, and fluorescent lights lit the room.

Morgan gasped. The place looked like a chemistry lab. Tables lined the sides, each filled with vials and tubes and liquids. Metal racks from floor to ceiling lined a corner and plastic bags were packed into the space.

"What is going on?"

"Meth," Tyler muttered.

Morgan blinked, reality settling over her. "This is a meth lab?"

He ran his hand across some equipment. "I haven't seen one this sophisticated here in the States. Most labs like these are only found in Mexico. This is quite the operation."

"No wonder the town had so much money to revitalize all the buildings."

Tyler grabbed a table and shoved the furniture in front of the door. "We've got to keep moving. Who knows how long it will be until they find us? The cave that Lindsey mentioned is our only hope."

Morgan nodded, anxiety digging its talons into her muscles again. The mere thought of the dark unknown they faced was enough to send her over the edge. But what other choice did they have? If they stayed here, they'd be discovered. Better to face her fears and have a smidgen of a chance at surviving.

Tyler squeezed her hand. "You ready for this?"

"Let's do it."

Tyler led her to a door on the far side of the room. He twisted the handle, revealing utter blackness on the other side. Stepping into the room felt like stepping into a black hole. A chill emanated from its depths.

Would this place end up being their grave?

No, don't think like that, Morgan told herself.

They could only see four feet in front of them—as far as the flashlight would shine. It seemed like Morgan had heard an old sermon illustration about this. About trusting God to lead you, that He'd give you enough light to see your next step but no more.

The darkness deepened, surrounding them like an abyss. If not for the single ray of light from Tyler's flashlight, Morgan might have given into her fears. Might have begged to turn around, to go back.

The space split. "Stay to the right," Tyler whispered. "That's what Lindsey said."

Was Lindsey leading them into a death trap? Were they trusting someone who could very well be in on their demise? But what choice did they have?

The passage narrowed. Morgan could no longer walk beside Tyler. Instead, she stayed a step behind. He never let go of her hand.

His grip on her was the only thing allowing her to keep her sanity.

Tyler shone his light upward. Bats nestled in the crevices there. "Maybe we're getting close to the end."

The end seemed a mere fantasy. This mountain had swallowed them, and they were at its mercy.

Tension pulled Morgan's stomach. Her heart beat out of control.

Shouldn't they be at the end by now? Were Rick's men already in the mine? Were they following them? What if they couldn't find help once they emerged?

Lord, help us...

Down, down. Deeper, deeper.

The chill intensified.

The passages squeezed.

The darkness suffocated.

"How are you doing, Morgan?" Tyler paused and shined the flashlight on her face. "You look like you're going to pass out."

"I'm fine. I can do this."

He pushed a hair back from her face. "I know you can." He kissed her forehead. "Let's keep moving. Not much farther."

That's what Morgan had thought an hour ago—at least it seemed like an hour ago. What if they got trapped in these caves? What would they do then?

Don't think like that. She couldn't.

She coughed. The cold already started to settle in her chest, burning her lungs every time she took a deep breath.

"I see a light ahead."

Her heart lifted as her gaze shot upward. There, in the distance, appeared a slice of gray. Could it really be the exit they'd been searching for?

A renewed energy surged through her. They'd reach the forest and walk until they found cell phone reception. Then law enforcement authorities would locate them and whisk them off to a safe location before they closed in on Rick's little cult.

Freedom was close enough that she could taste it.

The gray became brighter, bigger. The dankness of the cave cleared some as fresh, after-the-rain air flooded inside.

Only a few more feet.

Shadows of trees appeared, looming but welcoming. Had they actually done it? Had they made it out of Perfect alive?

Finally, they reached the hole, the so-called light at the end of the tunnel.

Their escape.

They stepped out just as the sun cracked over the horizon. Endless forest stared them down.

Now they just had to find help.

Morgan threw her arms around Tyler. "We did it."

Something clicked in the distance. An unnatural sound. A noise that made Morgan stiffen from her head to her toes.

Tyler edged himself in front of her and reached for his gun.

They waited. Tense. Breathless.

From behind a tree stepped Sheriff Lowe, his gun pointed directly at them.

Chapter Twenty-Six

Three deputies also slunk out from their forest cover. Each of their guns pointed at Tyler and Morgan. No, no, no, Morgan silently cried. This couldn't be happening. How had the sheriff known?

"Not so fast, City Slicker," Sheriff Lowe muttered to Tyler, stepping closer. "Put down that weapon or Ms. Blake dies right here and now."

"No one needs to get hurt." Tyler slowly lowered his hand to the ground and deposited his gun at the mouth of the cave.

"You thought you were going to get away? To ruin our plan that was months in the making?" The sheriff smirked. "I don't think so."

"How'd you know?" Morgan dared ask.

One of the deputies reached behind a tree and jerked Lindsey into their line of sight. Dirty tears streamed down the woman's face and, even in the gritty light, Morgan could see her black eye and busted lip.

"Lindsey…" Morgan wanted to reach out to the woman, to tell her everything would be okay. But would it be okay? Would any of them get out of this alive?

Tyler raised his hands in the air. "Let's talk this through."

The sheriff's eyes took on a dark gleam. "Too late for that. We got to get Ms. Blake back to town."

Tyler edged himself in front of her. "She's not going anywhere."

Sheriff Lowe smirked, stepping closer. "Mighty strong words for a man surrounded by guns."

Morgan coughed again, the cold seeming to solidify in her chest. "Sheriff Lowe, why don't you just let us go? The likelihood is we'll get lost in the forest anyway. Don't make this any worse for you."

His steely eyes glinted at her, their hollow depths reminding Morgan of the vast cave they'd just emerged from. "I wouldn't worry about things getting worse for me. I'd worry about things getting worse for you."

Morgan's throat tightened. She was going to end up in that massive grave, along with those other people who'd interfered with Perfect's grand scheme. Hope fizzled with each second. Morgan and Tyler's energy was spent. Even if they made a getaway, how far would they get in their exhaustion? Not far enough to be safe from the bullets that were sure to fly.

Sheriff Lowe pointed the gun at Tyler. "We'd kill you now, but the Almighty wants a word with you first."

The Almighty? Is that what people called Rick around here? Was there any hope of convincing his followers that he was no good, only out for his own purposes?

Tyler's jaw flexed. "The FBI knows where we are. You won't get away with this."

The FBI? That's right. They'd find them.

But would they find them in time?

Nudge them, Lord. Nudge them.

Sheriff Lowe nodded toward the distance. "We're going to get you two back to town. Just down that trail are our cars. Don't try anything funny or Lindsey gets a bullet in the head."

A deputy kneed Lindsey in the gut. She gasped, doubling over in pain. Morgan reached for her, but Tyler held her back. Tears burned Morgan's eyes.

Not Lindsey. Amber needed a mom. Lindsey needed a chance to claim her life for herself again.

Lord, how are we ever going to get out of this?

"No one needs to get hurt." Tyler, the voice of reason. He'd promised her the impossible. He'd promised to get her out of Perfect alive. "Why don't you leave Lindsey alone? Only a weak man would prey on someone defenseless."

A weak man. Like Braden. Like her stepdad. Like Rick.

"Go!" The sheriff shoved Tyler toward the trail. One of his deputies led the way. Morgan followed behind them. The sheriff pushed Lindsey to the next place in line.

They sloshed down the muddy trail, the ground still saturated from the storm earlier. Parts were steep, slippery, treacherous. Morgan's bones ached. Her muscles ached. Her chills deepened.

They marched toward the vehicles barely visible through the trees. Morgan stole a glance behind her. Lindsey. She looked broken, battered, and empty.

"We'll get you out of here, Lindsey. We'll get help."

She dragged her gaze up from the ground. "It's too late. Can't you see?"

"It's never too late." Even as she said the words, she wondered if she believed them. She had no idea how they would get out of this situation.

"Stop the chit chat," Sheriff Lowe growled. "Keep walking."

Morgan stepped across a rock. Landed wrong. Her ankle twisted. Pain screamed up her leg.

Tyler appeared beside her. "Are you okay?"

She ignored the tears that rushed to her eyes. "I'll be fine."

"Can you walk?"

"Let's see."

Tyler gently lifted her. As soon as Morgan put pressure on her ankle, intense pain ripped through her.

"What's going on here?" the sheriff asked.

"Morgan's hurt."

Sheriff Lowe scowled. "Carry her."

Tyler scooped her into his arms. She rested her head against his chest, tried to ward away the fear that hunted her at every turn.

When they reached the bottom of the path, Sheriff Lowe pointed with his Glock toward a sheriff's cruiser. "Put her in the backseat."

Morgan's grip around Tyler's neck tightened. "I want to stay with Tyler."

"Strict orders. You're not staying together. Now get in."

Tyler carried her toward the cruiser. His mouth went to her ear. "I'll find you, Morgan. I'll find you," he whispered. "I love you."

"I love you, too."

"Enough! Now, get in."

Tyler rested her in the backseat before taking a step back. She stole one last glance at Tyler and Lindsey as Sheriff Lowe climbed in the driver's seat and pulled away.

Morgan wrapped her arms over her chest, willing her teeth to stop chattering. Willing despair to loosen its grip. She'd fight to the end. She had to.

She coughed again. "Where are we going, sheriff?"

His gaze flickered to the rearview mirror as they bumped down the dirt road. "I'm not chatting with you, Ms. Blake."

She stared at the brightening gray of the forest. How far from Perfect were they? "I just asked where we were going."

"You'll find out soon enough."

She needed to keep him talking. She needed to somehow try and tap into his human side. "Could you turn the heat on back here?"

He grunted but flipped a switch in the front. Air began flowing through the vents on the floor. Maybe she could break through to him. Maybe.

"So how did The Almighty lure you out to Perfect, sheriff? Did he promise you wealth? Status? Power?"

"You don't know anything, Ms. Blake." His voice sounded tight, unyielding.

"I know more than you want to admit, don't I? How's that plan worked out for you? You don't have any of those things, do you? You only have what Joshua gives you. What kind of man lives like that? Depending on another man, bowing to his every whim, jumping when he says jump?"

His neck reddened. "It's not like that."

"Sure it is. This is no life. You're just a puppet."

"You think you know so much?" he hissed. "You have no idea what my life was like! Joshua's a good man. He's going to revolutionize this town. This state. This country. You're not going to ruin his plan."

"Why am I part of his plan?"

"You're the chosen one."

His words sent bone-shattering chills through her. "I don't want to be chosen."

"We don't always have choices."

"Sure we do."

He swung his head back and forth like a lead pendulum. "You'll see. Now stop talking. I knew you should have never been invited here in the first place."

Her skin prickled. "So all of this was planned? Why me?"

"I'm not answering any more of your questions, Ms. Blake. Do you take me for an idiot?"

"I'm just trying to understand."

They stopped in front of City Hall. Sheriff Lowe jerked her out of the car. Her ankle screamed under her weight. The sheriff didn't care. He pulled her behind him, hobbling, wincing with pain, tears flowing down her cheeks.

They approached the back door. Where was Tyler? Why wasn't the other sheriff's cruiser behind them? Where was everyone else? Were they okay?

The sheriff's grip on her arm felt like a clamp as he pulled her down stairs, toward the basement.

If Morgan was going to do something, she had to do it now.

She hesitated for just a second, long enough for the sheriff to get a step ahead of her. Then she jerked out of his grasp and shoved him until he tumbled down the stairs. She didn't waste any time. She turned on her heel and pulled herself up the steps. She had to get outside. Find a place to hide. Look for Tyler.

"Not so fast."

She looked up. Rick.

Fight or flight.

Before she could decide, Rick slapped her with his pistol, and her world went black.

Chapter Twenty-Seven

Tyler didn't like the fact that Morgan left in a different car.

He didn't like that they'd waited for a good five minutes before pulling away with Tyler in a separate car.

Lindsey stayed in a third car bringing up the rear.

Why were they making sure the cars took off at different times? What exactly were they planning, and how would Tyler get out of this one?

He soaked in the landscape around him, trying to formulate a plan, to guess their next move.

Where were they taking him? Where had they taken Morgan?

Tyler had to find Morgan before something happened to her. His friend with the FBI knew he was here. If they disappeared, the feds would come in. The question was… would they get here in time?

Joshua Sutherland needed to be stopped before more people got hurt. These people had been programmed. They'd come to depend on the cult leader for their every need. And, in the process, they'd put the man on a god-like pedestal.

This was more than he'd even bargained for. Because even worse than Joshua Sutherland's obvious love of power was the fact that the man was soulless. He'd kill people who tried to stop his plans.

That didn't make things look good for Tyler.

The driver craned his neck toward Tyler. "Don't make any moves or your girl will die. Understand?"

The deputy was probably in his early twenties and was as scrawny as Tyler had seen. But he had a gun and Tyler didn't. At the moment.

The car rolled along, through the forest, onto a highway. The deputy took the roads at a breakneck sped. Branches and stones that washed out from the storm littered the roadway, causing the deputy to jerk the wheel in last minute attempts to avoid a collision. The slick asphalt would make it easy for them to slide right off the side of this mountain or barrel into a rock wall.

At the last turn, Perfect came into sight. The streets seemed eerily quiet. Where was everyone? What were they planning?

The cruiser pulled to a stop in front of a mirrored building that seemed out of place in this town. The sign read City Hall.

The deputy put the car into park and stepped out. The sheriff emerged from a side door, rubbing his head as he walked toward them. He charged straight toward Tyler's door, yanked it open, and pulled Tyler out. He held onto Tyler's jacket, leering at him. "You weren't supposed to be here, Detective. You're messing our plans up."

Tyler gritted his teeth, resisting the urge to wipe away the spittle that flew from the sheriff's mouth. "I just want to find Morgan and take her home. That's all."

"That's not a part of our plan."

"What about Morgan's plan? Doesn't she have a say in this?"

Sheriff Lowe shook his head, a glint sparkling in his eyes. "Not right now. She will. In time."

Tyler didn't like the sound of that. "What are you going to do with me?"

"We're going to take a little walk." He raised his gun. "Now go. That way. Toward the woods."

Tyler did as the sheriff said, trying to time his move carefully. They walked down another trail. Water thundered in the background. The waterfall, Tyler realized.

Tyler swung around and kicked the gun out of the sheriff's hands. The sheriff slumped a moment, long enough for Tyler to sock him in the eye. Sheriff Lowe fell back, hitting the ground hard enough that it shook.

From somewhere unseen, a gun shot rang out.

Pain screamed through Tyler's arm.

And then he was falling backward—right down to the base of Widow Falls.

***

Morgan's head swirled. Pounded. Throbbed.

Her lungs ached.

She couldn't move, and blackness swallowed her whole.

Where was she? Why couldn't she turn over to relieve the ache in her body? Would the cold ever go away?

She plucked an eye open. Her eyelids felt held down with weights. Her arms heavy and frozen. Her world spun.

Finally, her eyes worked in unison, and the room came into focus. A plain room. She was on a table. Her arms and legs strapped down. Lights—off right now—hovered above her. A floor light shined softly in the corner.

Everything flashed back to her. Rick had caught her. Knocked her out.

And now she was here.

Where was Tyler? Was he still alive? What were they planning to do to her?

She tugged against her restraints. No use. Leather. Solid. Unyielding.

Why did her mind feel so fuzzy? Was she feverish?

No. Drugged. She'd been drugged.

Her head spun.

Rick. Joshua Sutherland. What was nagging at her?

She remembered the man who'd run against her stepfather. He'd been an underdog. Tall. Dark hair. Charismatic.

Rick's face danced in her mind. Slowly, his face morphed into…Gavin's?

Was Joshua Sutherland actually Gavin? No, Gavin was dead.

Dead.

She blacked out again.

***

Morgan wasn't sure how much time had passed when she came to again. This time, her thoughts felt clearer. Stable.

Someone appeared at her side. "I thought you'd never wake up."

She blinked. "Gavin. You're... alive."

"Yes. I'm sorry things have worked out the way they have. Our plan was supposed to run a much smoother course."

"You're Joshua Sutherland."

"You're a smart lady."

"Why are you doing this? Why don't you help me?"

He traced her cheek with his index finger. "I'd hoped we'd come to this point naturally. You're much more strong-willed than I assumed.

"Why are you doing this? Why did you lure me here?"

His face hardened. "Fifteen years ago, I ran against your father for a seat in the Senate. I was only thirty years old, and a young idealist. I ran as an independent, and had a strong but small following. I lost the election, and do you know what your father said to me? He said I was an embarrassment to politics, that I was the laughing stock of the political scene."

"That was a horrible thing to say."

"I decided that moment that I was going to succeed. And I was going to get revenge. I wrote this book and found amazing success. I found people who wanted to follow me. Then I knew I just had one more thing left to do on my list—to get revenge. What better revenge than to have the senator's daughter not only as a member of my little cult, but by my side as my wife, as the mother of my children."

"That will never happen. Never."

He smiled again. "We'll see about that."

"Besides, my stepfather doesn't care about me. I haven't spoken to him in months."

Gavin's face hardened. "Of course he cares."

"He's a bad person, Gavin. You're only going to gain him sympathy with voters when they hear what happened to me."

"By the time I'm done with you, Morgan, you're going to be a married woman who'd do anything for her husband. Happy. In love. It will be like a slap in the face to your stepfather."

"I'm never going to be by your side, Gavin. Never."

Gavin grinned, his eyes having a detached look about them. He stroked her hair away from her face. "I'm good at breaking people, Morgan."

"You'll never break me."

He grinned. "Don't be so sure. You get hungry enough, thirsty enough and you'll change your tune. When you start withdrawing from the meth, you'll start begging me for more. You'd do whatever you have to in order to get more."

Meth? Is that what they'd given her?

"Tyler will find me before that."

"Tyler is dead."

A cry caught her throat. "You're lying."

"He told Sheriff Lowe to tell you he loved you. He's sorry he died like your fiancé did."

Tears pushed themselves out.

He stood and pulled out a syringe. "Let the fun begin, beautiful. I'd really hoped to do this all the old fashioned way, but you're too stubborn and I've run out of time."

She screamed as the needle went into her skin. Then her world began to spin.

Chapter Twenty-Eight

When Morgan came to, the room was still spinning. Could it be true? Was Tyler really dead?

It couldn't be.

Not Tyler. Not when they'd been on the verge of something great and beautiful.

Tears pushed their way out and spilled down her cheeks.

This was her fault. She'd led Tyler here. He'd be safe if she hadn't been so foolhardy and stubborn.

Gavin appeared, leering before her with a gut-clenching smile on his face. He reached over, touched a button, and the lights over the table blared on. Their brightness blinded her. "Oh, you're not upset, are you?" He wiped her cheeks with the back of his hand. "I hate to see you cry."

"Just let me go before this gets any worse for you, Gavin." One last desperate plea. What else did she have to offer other than playing on his goodwill?

He grunted. "I like you, but I don't like you that much, Morgan. Besides, you like it here. You said so yourself."

"I like what you presented. But what you showed me about this town isn't real. It's all a façade. Just like you."

His eyes darkened. "Getting a little snobby, aren't you?"

"This is wrong, Gavin. It's all going to backfire."

"You don't know anything." His voice changed from carefree to gravelly. And, just as quickly as it changed, he snapped back into total control as he held up a needle, his eye glinting with pleasure. "You ready for another dose of candy? It's a handy-dandy mix that I came up with myself in order to achieve the desired outcome."

Meth. No, no more meth. Her throat felt so dry that she could hardly swallow. Her head throbbed.

But she wouldn't break. She hadn't stuck up for herself enough with Braden. She'd vowed to never let that happen again. That meant fighting until the end.

She licked her cracking lips. "You should just give up. Your plan's never going to work."

He tilted his head, arrogance seeping through his pores. "Just a couple of days ago you thought I was brilliant. Why the change of heart?"

"You can use power for good or evil. You've made your choice."

"Now, now, Morgan." He stroked her hair back from her face. "Your perception of good just isn't the same as mine. I help to provide a good life for the people here."

"At what cost? Dealing drugs? Killing anyone who gets in your way? That's not a good life. It's disgusting."

"I didn't realize you were this feisty. I like it." His finger traced the outline of her jaw. "Makes me fall in love with you even more."

She jerked back. "You don't know what love is."

He scowled and dropped his hand. "You'll see. I'm just sorry we have to do this the hard way."

He pushed the air from the needle.

She strained against her binds. It was useless. Morgan was trapped.

Gavin lowered the needle. Its tip pricked her skin, teasing her. She held her breath, waiting for the needle to plunge into her. Waiting for the narcotic to take hold of her thoughts again.

The door burst open. Morgan's head swung toward the sound. Tyler.

Or had Gavin already given her the meth? Was this just a hallucination?

Tyler aimed a gun at Gavin. "Put the needle down or I shoot."

Gavin's lips twisted in anger. "You are a persistent one. I thought the sheriff finished you off, but I can see he didn't do his duty."

"Put the needle down." Was that blood trickling down Tyler's shirt and forehead? What had happened to him?

Gavin appeared unflustered. He took a step closer to Tyler. "You know I have men all over this building."

Tyler shook his head. "Not anymore."

A moment of doubt flickered in Gavin's eyes. "Let's talk."

"There's nothing to talk about."

Gavin still held the needle. All it would take was one leap and he could jam it into Morgan's arm.

"You can be a part of this, you know. I can appoint you to a leadership position."

"The only thing I'm interested in is you putting that needle down. Now."

"Come on, can't we—"

A shot rang out. Gavin bent over in pain. Blood gushed from his hand.

Tyler crossed the room in two strides. His fist connected with Gavin's jaw and sent him sprawling to the floor. The needle scattered across the ground.

Before Gavin could stand, Tyler pulled the straps off Morgan's wrists and ankles. "Are you okay?"

"Now I am."

He lifted her from the table and placed her in a chair against the wall. He jerked Gavin from the ground. The man spewed hate as Tyler manhandled him. Tyler laid him on the table and strapped his arms down.

"I feel sorry for you, Gavin. You're not a man. Real men don't manipulate people in order to get their respect. They respect people and get respect in return." He jerked the last strap tight enough for Gavin to sneer in pain.

He rushed to Morgan and gathered her in his arms. "Can you walk?"

She shook her head. "Not fast."

"I've got you." He burst into the hallway. Empty. "Where is everyone?"

He moved quickly toward the back door. "I tied them up. But this whole town is crazy. Who knows what other obstacles wait ahead."

He took the stairs by two. "Not much longer."

Tyler darted toward the exit. He shoved the door open, ran across the sidewalk, and slid her into a waiting sheriff's cruiser. Less than thirty seconds later, he cranked the engine, locked the doors and squealed away.

Morgan leaned against the door, the drugs obviously still in her system. Her muscles felt like jelly. Her mind raced.

"Get down. I don't know what's waiting for us up here."

Morgan did as he said and slumped onto the floor. "How'd you get the car?"

"I knocked out the deputy and took his keys." The car accelerated. "Uh oh."

"What?"

"There's a crowd ahead. A big crowd. Most of the town, it looks like."

Tyler didn't slow. Morgan closed her eyes, praying for a good outcome.

Move, move! She silently urged.

"Here goes nothing," Tyler muttered.

Lord, help us all.

Morgan tensed, waiting to feel the thumps, cries of outrage, of pain.

Instead, she heard nothing. The car accelerated.

Finally, she plucked an eye open.

"You did it?"

"They moved," Tyler explained. "Thank goodness, they moved."

They sped away from Perfect and toward help.
They'd made it out alive. Thank God, they'd made it
out alive.

Chapter Twenty-Nine

Morgan leaned back into her couch and into Tyler's arms. She snuggled against him, her eyes fastened on the TV. The scene there seemed surreal yet real. Like a dream or a nightmare, but it was neither. The situation on TV was reality.

Three days had passed since they escaped Perfect. After breaking through the zombie-like crowd, they'd driven as fast and hard as they could until they reached the interstate—and a cell phone signal. They'd then called Tyler's friend with the FBI, who'd informed them that they already had men on the way.

A standoff had been going on in the town since then. The FBI, state police, and DEA had all surrounded Perfect, trying to coax people into surrendering. The national news picked up on the story and coverage had been nearly nonstop. One of the biggest cult stories since Waco, Texas.

Soon enough they'd find out about Morgan's role in the town's demise. The press would start calling, asking for interviews, digging into her past. Morgan could handle the media scrutiny—as long as Tyler was by her side. And since he'd already volunteered to be her personal bodyguard for as long as necessary, she had nothing to worry about.

The reporter on the screen turned toward the camera. "We've just gotten word that the cult's leader, Joshua Sutherland, has been found dead in the town's City Hall building. Sutherland apparently went by the name Gavin Antoine. He had a failed senate bid in Virginia more than a decade ago and went on to write several best-selling self-help books. Those books helped to broaden his scope of influence and attracted a following…"

Yep, Gavin had persuaded people to move to Perfect. After they got there, he'd made sure he controlled their jobs, their finances, their everything. He held mandatory meetings every week where he guilted people into doing his work. Rick had been his right-hand man.

"Enough yet?" Tyler asked.

Morgan nodded, her emotions a mix of grief and relief; of peace yet sadness.

Tyler raised the remote and flipped off the TV. "At least Lindsey and Amber are okay. Cade told me that Lindsey's twin was beside herself when she heard what had happened. I'm hoping they're having a happy reunion right now."

"Poor Amber. I can't believe they were using her as a pawn the whole time." Rick had taken her into hiding, all the while knowing her disappearance would pull on Morgan's heartstrings and keep her in town longer. The girl was safe now. She'd probably have to have a lot of counseling, but she would get past this. So would Lindsey.

"If there's one thing I've learned it's that things are hardly ever as perfect as they seem." Towns, relationships, people. Wasn't it the cracks and imperfections that made things beautiful, though? The trying, bruising moments when your humanity shone through?

My strength is made perfect in weakness.

Yes it was, Morgan thought. Everything she'd been through in life had been necessary to get her where she was today.

"You can say that again." Tyler kissed the back of her head. "Except for you, you know."

She stole a glance at him. "I'm nowhere near perfect. I've spent my life trying to be, though. I've covered up or ignored the less than appealing aspects of my life. It hasn't been until I talked about them that I've felt whole, though. Real. Is that weird?"

Tyler smiled and wiped a hair behind her ear. "Not at all. What's that saying? The truth will set you free? It's the hard times in life that makes us who we are."

He stood, grabbed Morgan's hand and led her to the second story deck that overlooked a peaceful Atlantic Ocean. Colors of the sunset smeared in the sky, a lovely pastel blur that seemed to represent everything peaceful.

Tyler blanketed her in his arms. Why did it take Morgan so long to realize that true love had been staring her in the face month after month? She shoved those questions aside. The important thing was that she had realized it now. With Tyler, her heart felt as serene as the sunset.

"What are you thinking about?"

She turned to face him. "I'm thinking that I'm thankful for the past because everything that happened led me to you."

A smile slowly cracked over his face. "That brings up something that I've been wanting to talk you to about."

"What's that?"

"Marrying me."

Her heart fluttered, yet never lost the deep, rooted feeling she had whenever Tyler was around. "You're asking?"

He dropped down to one knee, reached into his pocket, and emerged with a ring. The diamond glinted in the fading sunlight. "I am."

"I'll say yes on one condition."

His eye sparkled, swirled, as he gazed at her. "Anything."

"We can't go to the mountains on our honeymoon. Or spelunking. Ever."

Tyler laughed. As he stood and looked into Morgan's eyes, his chuckle faded, replaced by a huskiness that tingled Morgan's toes. "Anything for you."

Morgan couldn't stop the grin that spread over her face. "Then yes."

He wrapped his arms around and twirled her in a circle, letting out a whoop. When he set her down, his warm gaze locked on hers. "How about tomorrow?"

Morgan blinked in surprise and delight. "Tomorrow? As in, get married tomorrow?"

"Why waste any time? It's not like we just met."

"Getting married when I'm thirty days away from a major deadline may not be the best idea."

"I think it's a great idea. I can take some vacation time. We can hole ourselves up in a little cabin for awhile where you can—"

"Write?"

He shrugged sheepishly. "Exactly. Where you can write."

She let the idea settle in her mind before slowly nodding. "Okay. Let's do it. As soon as possible. I don't need a big wedding."

His eyes lit. "You mean it?"

"Of course I mean it. I have no doubts about you, Tyler Carson. None."

"That makes me a very happy man. Very happy, Morgan Blake." His lips covered hers and, for a moment, the world disappeared. When the kiss dwindled, they stood silently watching the waves break on the shoreline.

"How's the story coming anyway?" Tyler asked.

"I actually know exactly where I need to go with it now. And when my publisher realizes the great publicity angle I have, I think they're going to be happy. Even if I do turn the book in a little later than intended."

"Good. I'm glad the muse found you again."

She was too. All it had taken was one little tweak in her opening sentence to set the direction of her entire story.

I remember the day darkness slithered into my town. *Like a boa constructor, evil wrapped itself around the very heart of our existence and squeezed until all signs of life were gone.*

Letter to Readers:

The Trouble with Perfect originally released in 2004. The book was one of the first novels I had published. Since then, I've had six other books release and grown in my craft. So when *The Trouble with Perfect* went out of print with its first publisher, I decided to revisit the story. I was pleasantly surprised to get wrapped up in the eerie little town of Perfect. Just a few tweaks, I thought. A few tweaks turned into a couple of months of revisions, but I'm so glad I was able to take Morgan and Tyler's story and fine-tune it.

I love the mountains, and I love West Virginia. I've spent a lot of time there exploring and whitewater rafting. Almost anywhere you go in the state you can see reminders of God's beautiful and vast creations. But, as with any story's origin, I began asking myself, "What if…" That's when *The Trouble with Perfect* was born.

I hope you enjoyed *The Trouble with Perfect*. Whatever you do, don't let it stop you from enjoying Wild, Wonderful West Virginia if you ever have the chance.

43256382R00149

Made in the USA
Lexington, KY
23 July 2015